"You Might Very Well Be The Hottest Male On The Planet, But I Am Not Willing To Be Your Latest Conquest."

Her hands clenched into fists and socked against his chest. For emphasis. And maybe to unleash some frustration. He didn't move an iota.

For who knew what ill-advised reason, he reached out, but then wisely stopped shy of her face. "Is it so difficult to believe you intrigue me and I simply want to unwrap the rest of you?"

"Yeah. It is." She crossed her arms to prevent any more unloading of frustration. His chest was as hard as his head. And other places. "You're feeling deprived. Go find one of the women who text messaged you earlier in the car, and scratch your itch with her, because I'm not sleeping with you."

A smile curved his mouth, but the opposite of humor flashed through his steely gaze. "In case it's slipped your mind, I'm married. The only person I'll be sleeping with for the next six months is my wife."

D0324590

Dear Reader,

Once upon a time there was a reader who believed so strongly in the magic of romance novels, she dreamed of creating one of her own. She put pen to paper and, later, fingers to the keyboard, and like the very best of spells, words wove together and became people, settings, conflict, emotion and finally, a story complete with a happily-ever-after. One day, after many missed carriages and a distinct lack of awesome shoes, her (very young and beautiful) fairy godmother called. She waved her wand and said the magic words: "This is Harlequin. We'd like to publish your book."

As I'm sure you guessed, I'm that reader, and because you're holding this book in your hands, I'm also now a published author. Harlequin chose this story as the winner of the 2011 So You Think You Can Write competition, which has indeed been the most magical of journeys, and I'm so excited to be a part of the Harlequin family.

I adore this story about a laid-back Southern hero who lacks only a spitfire heroine to keep him on his toes. Lucas and Cia are two of my favorite fictional people and I hope you enjoy them as much as I enjoyed writing them.

I love to hear from readers—after all, I wrote this book for you! Please visit me at www.katcantrell.com.

Kat Cantrell

KAT CANTRELL

MARRIAGE WITH BENEFITS

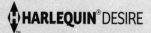

If you purchased this book without a cover you should be aware that this book is stolen property. It was reported as "unsold and destroyed" to the publisher, and neither the author nor the publisher has received any payment for this "stripped book."

Recycling programs
for this product may
not exist in your area.

ISBN-13: 978-0-373-73225-8

MARRIAGE WITH BENEFITS

Copyright © 2013 by Katrina Williams

All rights reserved. Except for use in any review, the reproduction or utilization of this work in whole or in part in any form by any electronic, mechanical or other means, now known or hereafter invented, including xerography, photocopying and recording, or in any information storage or retrieval system, is forbidden without the written permission of the publisher, Harlequin Enterprises Limited, 225 Duncan Mill Road, Don Mills, Ontario M3B 3K9, Canada.

This is a work of fiction. Names, characters, places and incidents are either the product of the author's imagination or are used fictitiously, and any resemblance to actual persons, living or dead, business establishments, events or locales is entirely coincidental.

This edition published by arrangement with Harlequin Books S.A.

For questions and comments about the quality of this book, please contact us at CustomerService@Harlequin.com.

® and TM are trademarks of Harlequin Enterprises Limited or its corporate affiliates. Trademarks indicated with ® are registered in the United States Patent and Trademark Office, the Canadian Trade Marks Office and in other countries.

Printed in U.S.A.

KAT CANTRELL

read her first Harlequin novel in third grade and has been scribbling in notebooks since she learned to spell. What else would she write but romance? She majored in literature, officially with the intent to teach, but somehow ended up buried in middle management at Corporate America, until she became a stay-at-home mom and full-time writer.

Kat, her husband and their two boys live in north Texas. When she's not writing about characters on the journey to happily-ever-after, she can be found at a soccer game, watching the TV show *Friends* or listening to 80s music.

Kat was the 2011 Harlequin So You Think You Can Write winner and a 2012 RWA Golden Heart finalist for best unpublished series contemporary manuscript.

This one is for you, Mom.
Thanks for sharing your love of books with me.

One

Other single, twenty-five-year-old women dreamed of marriageable men and fairy-tale weddings, but Dulciana Allende dreamed of a divorce.

And Lucas Wheeler was exactly the man to give it to her.

Cia eyed her very male, very blond and very broad-shouldered target across the crowded reception hall. The display of wealth adorning the crush between her and Lucas bordered on garish. A doddering matron on her left wore a ring expensive enough to buy a year's worth of groceries for the women's shelter where Cia volunteered.

But then, if Cia had the natural ability to coax that kind of cash out of donors, she wouldn't be here in the middle of a Dallas society party, where she clearly did not belong, about to put plan B into action.

There was no plan C.

She knocked back the last swallow of the froufrou drink some clueless waiter had shoved into her hand. After she'd put considerable effort into securing a last-minute invitation to Mrs. Wheeler's birthday party, the least she could do was play along and drink whatever lame beverage the Black Gold Club pretended had alcohol in it. If she pulled off this negotiation, Mrs. Wheeler would be her future mother-in-law, and Cia did want to make a favorable impression.

Well, Mrs. Wheeler was also her future ex-mother-in-law, so perhaps the impression didn't matter overly much.

A guy near the bar tried to catch her eye, but she kept walking. Tonight, she cared about only one man and, conveniently, he stood next to his mother greeting guests. Cia's unfamiliar heels and knee-binding slim dress slowed her trek across the room. Frustrating but fortunate, since a giraffe on roller blades had her beat in the grace department.

"Happy birthday, Mrs. Wheeler." Cia shook the hand of the stylish, fifty-something woman and smiled. "This is a lovely party. Dulciana Allende. Pleased to meet you."

Mrs. Wheeler returned the smile. "Cia Allende. My, where has the time gone? I knew your parents socially. Such a tragedy to lose them at the same time." She clucked maternally.

Cia's smile faltered before she could catch it. Of course Mrs. Wheeler had known her parents. She just didn't know Cia's stomach lurched every time someone mentioned them in passing.

"Lucas, have you met Cia?" Mrs. Wheeler drew him forward. "Her grandfather owns Manzanares Communications."

Cia made eye contact with the man she planned to marry and fell headfirst into the riptide of Lucas Wheeler in the flesh. He was so…everything. Beautiful. Dynamic. Legendary. Qualities the internet couldn't possibly convey via fiber-optic lines.

"Miz Allende." Lucas raised her hand to his lips in an old-fashioned—and effective—gesture. And set off a whole different sort of lurch, this time someplace lower. *No, no, no.* Attraction was not acceptable. Attraction unsettled her, and when she was unsettled, she came out with swords drawn.

"Wheeler." She snatched her hand from his in a hurry. "I don't believe I've ever met anyone who so closely resembles a Ken doll."

His mother, bless her, chatted with someone else and thankfully didn't hear Cia's mouth working faster than her brain. Social niceties weren't her forte, especially when it came to men. How had she fooled herself into believing she could do this?

Lucas didn't blink. Instead, he swept her from head to toe with a slow, searching glance that teased a hot flush along her skin. With an amused arch to one brow, he said, "Lucky for me I've got one up on Ken. I bend all sorts of ways."

Her breath gushed out in a flustered half laugh. She did not want to like him. Or to find him even remotely attractive. She'd picked him precisely because she assumed she wouldn't. As best as she could tell from the articles she'd read, he was like the Casanovas she'd dated in college, pretty and shallow.

Lucas was nothing but a good-time guy who happened to be the answer to saving hundreds of women's lives. This marriage would help so many people, and just in case that wasn't enough of a reason for him to agree to her deal, she'd come armed with extra incentives.

That reassuring thought smoothed out the ragged hitch to her exhale. Refocusing, she pasted on a smile. His return smile bolstered her confidence. Her business with Lucas Wheeler was exactly that—business. And if she knew anything, it was business. If only her hands would stop shaking. "To be fair, you do look better in a suit than Ken."

"Now, I'd swear that sounded like a compliment." He leaned in a little and cocked his head. "If our parents knew each other, how is it we've never met?"

His whiskey-drenched voice stroked every word with a lazy Texas drawl that brought to mind cowboys, long, hard rides in the saddle and heat. She met his smoky blue eyes squarely and locked her knees. "I don't get out much."

"Do you dance?" He nodded to the crowded square of teak hardwood, where guests swayed and flowed to the beat of the jazz ensemble playing on a raised stage.

"Not in public."

Something flittered across his face, and she had the impression he'd spun a private-dance scenario through his head. Lips pursed, he asked, "Are you sure we haven't met before?"

"Positive."

And Cia wished circumstances had conspired differently to continue their mutual lack of acquaintance. Men like Lucas—expert at getting under a woman's skin right before they called it quits—were hazardous to someone who couldn't keep her heart out of it, no matter what she promised herself.

But she'd make any sacrifice necessary to open a new women's shelter and see her mother's vision realized. Even marrying this man who radiated sensuality like a vodka commercial laced with an aphrodisiac. "We're only meeting now because I have a proposition for you."

A slow, lethal smile spilled across his face. "I like propositions."

Her spine tingled, and that smile instantly became the thing she liked least about Lucas Wheeler. It was too dangerous, and he didn't hesitate to wield it. *Dios,* did she detest being disconcerted. Especially by a man she hoped to marry platonically. "It's not that kind of proposition. Not even close. I cannot stress enough how far removed it is from what that look in your eye says you assume."

"Now I'm either really interested or really not interested." Smoothly, he tapped his lips with a square-cut nail and sidled closer, invading her space and enveloping her with his woodsy, masculine scent. "I can't decide which."

The man had the full package, no question. Women didn't throw themselves at his feet on a regular basis because he played a mean hand of Texas hold 'em.

"You're interested," she told him and stepped back a healthy foot. He couldn't afford not to be, according to her meticulous research. She'd sifted through dozens of potential marriage candidates and vetted them all through her best friend, Courtney, before settling on this one.

Of course, she hadn't counted on him somehow hitting spin cycle on her brain.

"So," she continued, "I'll get right to it. Hundreds of women suffer daily from domestic abuse, and my goal is to help them escape to a place where they can build new lives apart from the men using them for punching bags. The shelters in this area are packed to the brim, and we need another one. A big one. An expensive one. That's where you come in."

They'd already taken in more bodies than the existing shelter could hold, and it was only a matter of time before the occupancy violation became known. Lucas Wheeler was going to change the future.

A shutter dropped over Lucas's expression, and he shook his head. "My money is not subject to discussion. You're barking up the wrong sugar daddy."

"I don't want your money. I have my own. I just have to get my hands on it so I can build the shelter my way, without any benefactors, investors or loans."

She flinched a little at her tone. *What* about this man brought out her claws?

"Well, darlin'. Sounds like I'm unnecessary, then. If you decide to go in the other direction with your proposition, feel free to look me up." Lucas edged away, right into the sights of a svelte socialite in a glittery, painted-on dress, who'd clearly been waiting for the most eligible male in the place to reject her competition.

"I'm not finished." Cia crossed her arms and followed him, shooting a well-placed glare at Ms. Socialite. She wisely retreated to the bar. "The money is tied up in my trust fund. In order to untie it, I have to turn thirty-five, which is nearly a decade away. Or get married. If my husband files for divorce, as long as the marriage lasts at least six months, the money's mine. You're necessary since I'd like you to be that husband."

Lucas chuckled darkly and, to his credit, didn't flinch. "Why is every woman obsessed with money and marriage? I'm actually disappointed you're exactly like everyone else."

"I'm nothing like everyone else." Other women tried to keep husbands. She wanted to get rid of one as soon as possible, guaranteeing she controlled the situation, not the other way around. Getting rid of things before they sank barbs into her heart was the only way to fly. "The difference here is you need me as much as I need you. The question is can you admit it?"

He rolled his eyes, turning them a hundred different shades of blue. "That's a new angle. I'm dying to hear this one."

"Sold any big-ticket properties lately, Wheeler?"

Instantly, he stiffened underneath his custom-made suit, stretching it across his shoulders, and she hated that she noticed. He was well built. So what? She had absolute control of her hormones, unlike his usual female companions. His full package wasn't going to work on her.

"What's real estate got to do with your trust fund?"

She shrugged. "You're in a bit of a fix. You need to shore up your reputation. I need a divorce. We can help each other, and I'll make it well worth your while."

No other single male in the entire state fit her qualifications, and, honestly, she didn't have the nerve to approach another stranger. She scared off men pretty quickly, which saved her a lot of heartache, but left her with zero experience in working her feminine wiles. That meant she had to offer something her future husband couldn't refuse.

"Hold up, sweetheart." Lucas signaled a waiter, snagged two drinks from the gilded tray and jerked his head. "You've got my attention. For about another minute. Let's take this outside. I have a sudden desire for fresh air. And double-plated armor for that shotgun you just stuck between my ribs."

Lucas could almost feel the bite of that shotgun as he turned and deftly sidestepped through the crowd.

His brother, Matthew, worked a couple of local businessmen, no doubt on the lookout for a possible new client, and glanced up as Lucas passed. The smarmy grin on Matthew's face said volumes about Lucas's direction and the woman with him.

Lucas grinned back. Had to keep up appearances, after all. A hard and fast quickie on the shadowed balcony did smack of his usual style, but it was the furthest thing from his mind.

The gorgeous—and nutty—crusader with the intriguing curtain of dark hair followed him to the terrace at the back of the club. By the time he'd set down the pair of drinks, she'd already sailed through the door without waiting for him to open it.

Lucas sighed and retrieved the glasses, seriously considering downing both before joining the Spanish curveball on the balcony. But his mama had raised him better than that.

"Drink?" He offered one to Cia, and surprise, surprise, she took it.

Twenty-five stories below, a siren cut through the muted sounds of downtown Dallas, and cool March air kissed the back of his hot neck. If nothing else, he'd escaped the stuffy ballroom. But he had a hunch he'd left behind the piranhas in favor of something with much sharper teeth.

"Thanks. Much better than the frilly concoction I got last round." She sipped the bourbon and earned a couple of points with him. "So. Now that I have your attention, listen carefully. This is strictly a business deal I'm offering. We get married in name only, and in six months, you file for divorce. That's it. Six months is plenty of time to rebuild your reputation, and I get access to my trust fund afterward."

Reputation. If only he could laugh and say he didn't care what other people thought of him.

But he was a Wheeler. His great-great-grandfather had founded Wheeler Family Partners over a century ago and almost single-handedly shaped the early north Texas landscape. Tradition, family and commerce were synonymous with the Wheeler name. Nothing else mattered.

"You're joking, right?" He snorted as a bead of sweat slid between his shoulder blades. "My reputation is fine. I'm not hard up for a magic wand, thanks."

The little bundle of contradictions in the unrevealing, yet oddly compelling, dress peered up steadily through sooty lashes. "Really, Wheeler? You're gonna play that card? If this fake marriage is going to work, know this. I don't kowtow to the Y chromosome. I won't hesitate to tell you how it is or how it's going to be. Last, and not least, I do my research. You lost the contract on the Rose building yesterday, so don't pretend your clients aren't quietly choosing to do business with another firm where the partners keep their pants zipped. Pick a different card."

"I didn't know she was married."

Brilliant, Wheeler. Astound her with some more excuses. Better yet, tell her how great Lana had been because she only called occasionally, suggested low-key, out-of-the-way places to eat and never angled to stay overnight. In hindsight, he'd been a class A idiot to miss the signs.

"But she was. I'm offering you some breathing room. A chance to put distance and time between you and the scandal, with a nice, stable wife who will go away in six months. I insist on a prenup. I'm not asking you to sleep with me. I'm not even asking you to like me. Just sign a piece of paper and sign another one in six months."

Breathing room. Funny. He'd never been less able to breathe than right now. His temple started throbbing to the muted beat of the music playing on the other side of the glass.

Even a fake marriage would have ripples, and no way could it be as easy as a couple of signatures. Mama would have a coronary if he so much as breathed the word *divorce* after giving her a daughter-in-law. She'd dang near landed in the hospital after her first daughter-in-law died, even though Amber and Matthew had barely been married a year.

A divorce would set his gray-sheep status in stone, and he'd been killing himself to reverse the effects of his monumental lapse in judgment with Lana. Why eliminate what little progress he'd achieved so far?

The other temple throbbed. "Darlin', you're not my type. Conquistador Barbie just doesn't do it for me."

The withering scowl she leveled at him almost pared back his skin. "That's the beauty of this deal. There's no chance of being tempted to turn this physical. No messy ties. It's a business agreement between respected associates with a finite term. I can't believe you're balking at this opportunity."

Because it was *marriage*. Marriage was a "someday" thing, a commitment he'd make way, way, way in the future, once he found the right woman. He'd be giving this stranger his name, sharing his daily life with her.

And of course, he'd be married, the opposite of single. "For the record, I'm wounded to learn my temptation factor is zero. It can't be as simple as you're making it out to be. What if someone finds out it's not real? Will you still get the money?"

"No one will find out. I'm not going to tell anyone. You're not going to tell anyone. We only have to fake being madly in love once or twice around other people so my grandfather buys it. Behind closed doors, we can do our own thing."

Madly in love. Faking that would be a seriously tall order when he'd never been so much as a tiny bit in love. "Why can't you have the money unless you get divorced? That's the weirdest trust clause I've ever heard."

"Nosy, aren't you?"

He raised a brow. "Well, now, darlin', you just proposed to me. I'm entitled to a few questions."

"My grandfather is old-fashioned. When my parents died…" Her lips firmed into a flat line. "He wants me to be taken care of, and in his mind, that means a husband. I'm supposed to fall in love and get married and have babies, not get a divorce. The money is a safety net in case the husband bails, one I put considerable effort into convincing my grandfather to include."

"Your grandfather has met you, right?" He grinned. "Five minutes into our acquaintance, and I would never make the mistake of thinking you can't look after yourself. Why thirty-five? You don't strike me as one to blow your trust fund on cocaine and roulette."

"I donated all the money I inherited from my parents to the shelter where I work," she snapped, as if daring him to say something—anything—about it. "And don't go thinking I'm looking for handouts. My grandfather set up the trust and deposits the considerable interest directly into my bank account. I have more than enough to live on, but not enough to build a shelter. He's hoping I'll lose enthusiasm for battered women by thirty-five."

"Well, that's obviously not going to happen."

"No. And I don't enjoy being manipulated into marriage." She tightened the lock of her crossed arms. "Look, it's not like I'm asking you to hurt puppies or put your money into a pyramid scheme. This is going to save lives. Women who suffer domestic abuse have nowhere to go. Most of them don't have much education and have to work to feed their kids. Consider it charity. Or are you too selfish?"

"Hey now. I'm on the Habitat for Humanity board. I tithe my ten percent. Give me a break."

Good button to push, though, because against his will, wheels started turning.

Six months wasn't too much of a sacrifice for the greater good, was it? Abuse was a terrible evil, and a charity that helped abuse victims was well worth supporting. He took in Cia's fierce little form and couldn't help but wonder what had sparked all that passion. Did she reserve it for crusading or did she burn this brightly in other one-on-one situations, too?

Through the glass separating the balcony from the ballroom, he watched his grandparents slow dance in the midst of his parents' friends. Could he make this fake marriage work and protect his family from divorce fallout at the same time? He couldn't deny how far a nice, stable wife might go toward combating his problems with Lana's husband. Probably not a bad idea to swear off women for a while anyway. Maybe if he kept Cia away from his family as much as possible, Mama would eventually forget about the absentee daughter-in-law.

No. No way. This whole setup gave him hives.

Mama would never let him keep a wife squirreled away, no matter what he intended. Cia could find someone else to marry, and together he and Matthew would straighten out the kinks in Wheeler Family Partners' client list. "As…interesting as all this sounds, afraid I'll have to pass."

"Not so fast." Her gaze pierced him with a prickly, no-nonsense librarian thing. "I'm trusting you with this information. Don't disappoint me or you'll spend the next six months tied up in court. My grandfather is selling the cell phone division of Manzanares and moving the remainder of the business to a smaller facility. I'm sure you're familiar with his current location?"

Four buildings surrounding a treed park, centrally located and less than ten years old. Designed by Brown & Worthington in an innovative, award-winning Mediterranean/modern architectural mix. Approximately three million square feet with access to the DART light-rail.

"Slightly."

"My grandfather would be thrilled to give the exclusive sales contract for the complex to my husband."

She waited, but calculations had already scrolled through his head.

The commission on Manzanares beat the Rose building by quadruple. And the prestige—it could lead to other clients for Wheeler Family Partners, and instead of being the Wheeler who'd screwed up, he'd be the family's savior.

Out of nowhere, the fifty-pound weight sitting on his chest

rolled off. "If I went so far as to entertain this insane idea, can I call you Dulciana?"

"Not if you expect me to answer. My name is Cia, which, incidentally, sounds nothing like *darling,* so take note. Are you in or out?"

He had to tell her *now?* Evidently Cia did not subscribe to the Lucas Wheeler Philosophy of Life—anything worth doing was worth taking the time to do right. "Why me?"

"You may play the field well and often, but research shows you treat women with respect. That's important to me. Also, everything I've read says you'll keep your word, a rare commodity. I can't be the one to file for divorce so I have to trust you will."

Oddly, her faith touched him. But the feeling didn't sit well. "Don't you have a boyfriend or some other hapless male in your life you can railroad into this?"

"There's no one else. In my experience, men have one primary use." She let her gaze rove over him suggestively, and the atmosphere shifted from tense to provocative. Hidden terrace lighting played over her features, softening them, and that unrevealing dress dangled the promise of what she'd hidden under it.

Then she finished the sentiment. "To move furniture."

That's why this exotically beautiful woman didn't have a boyfriend stashed somewhere. Any guy sniffing around Miz Allende had to want it bad enough to work for it. Nobody was worth that much effort, not even this ferocious little crusader with the mismatched earrings who'd waltzed into the Black Gold Club and walked across the room with a deliberate, slow gait he'd thoroughly enjoyed watching. "You win. I'll call you Cia."

Her brows snapped together. "Throw down your hand, Wheeler. You've got nothing to lose and everything to gain by marrying me. Yes or no?"

She was all fire and passion, and it was a dirty shame she seemed hell-bent on keeping their liaison on paper. But he usually liked his women uncomplicated and easygoing, so treating this deal as business might be the better way to go.

He groaned. At what point had he started to buy into this lunatic idea of a fake-but-pretend-it's-real marriage to a woman he'd just met? Call him crazy, but he'd always imagined having lots of sex with the woman he eventually married…way, way, way in the future.

If he pursued her, he'd have to work hard to get Miz Allende into bed, which didn't sound appealing in the least, and the deal would be difficult enough.

Business only, then, in exchange for a heap of benefits.

The Manzanares contract lay within his grasp. He couldn't pass up the chance to revitalize his family's business. Yeah, Matthew would be right there, fighting alongside Lucas no matter what, but he shouldn't have to be. The mess belonged to Lucas alone, and a way to fix it had miraculously appeared.

"No," he said.

"No?" Cia did a fair impression of a big-mouth bass. "As in you're turning me down?"

"As in I don't kowtow to the X chromosome. You want to do business, we'll do it in my office tomorrow morning. Nine sharp." Giving him plenty of time to do a little reconnaissance so he could meet his future wife-slash-business-partner toe-to-toe. Wheelers knew how to broker a deal. "With lawyers, without alcohol, and darlin', don't be late."

Her face went blank, and the temperature dropped at least five degrees. She nodded once. "Done."

Hurricane Cia swept toward the door, and he had no doubt the reprieve meant he stood in the eye of the storm. No problem. He'd load up on storm-proof, double-plated armor in a heartbeat if it meant solving all his problems in one shot.

Looked like he was going to make an effort after all.

Two

Cia had been cooling her heels a full twenty minutes when Lucas strolled into the offices of Wheeler Family Partners LLC at 9:08 a.m. the next morning. Renewed anger ate through another layer of her stomach lining. She'd had to ask Courtney to cover her responsibilities at the shelter to attend this meeting, and the man didn't have the courtesy to be on time. He'd pay for that. Especially after he'd ordered her not to be late in that high-handed, deceptively lazy drawl.

"Miz Allende." Lucas nodded as if he often found women perched on the edge of the leather couch in the waiting area. He leaned on the granite slab covering the receptionist's desk. "Helena, can you please reschedule the nine-thirty appraisal and send Kramer the revised offer I emailed you? Give me five minutes to find some coffee, and then show Miz Allende to my office."

The receptionist smiled and murmured her agreement. Her eyes widened as Cia stalked up behind Lucas. The other women often found on Lucas's couch must bow to the master's bidding.

Cia cleared her throat, loudly, until he faced her. "I've got other activities on my agenda today, Wheeler. Skip the coffee, and I'll follow *you* to your office."

Inwardly, she cringed. Not only were her feminine wiles out of practice, she'd let Lucas get to her. She couldn't keep being so witchy or he'd run screaming in the other direction long before realizing the benefits of marrying her.

If only he'd stop being so…Lucas for five minutes, maybe she'd be able to bite her tongue.

Lucas didn't call her on it, though. He just stared at her, evaluating. Shadows under his lower lashes deepened the blue of his irises, and fatigue pulled at the sculpted lines of his face. Her chin came up. Carousing till all hours, likely. He probably always looked like that after rolling out of some socialite's bed, where he'd done everything but sleep.

Not her problem. Not yet anyway.

Without a blink, he said, "Sure thing, darlin'. Helena, would you mind?"

He smiled gratefully at the receptionist's nod and ushered Cia down a hall lined with a lush Turkish rug over espresso hardwood. Pricey artwork hung on the sage walls and lent to the moneyed ambience of the office. Wheeler Family Partners had prestige and stature among the elite property companies in Texas, and she prayed Lucas cared as much as she assumed he did about preserving his heritage, or her divorce deal would be dead on arrival.

She had to convince him to say yes. Her mother's tireless efforts on behalf of abused women must reach fruition.

They passed two closed doors, each with name plaques reading Robert Wheeler and Andrew Wheeler, respectively. The next door was open. Lucas's office reflected the style of the exterior. Except he filled his space with a raw, masculine vibe the second he crossed the threshold behind her, crowding her and forcing her to retreat.

Flustered, she dropped into the wingback chair closest to

the desk. She had to find her footing here. But how did one go about bloodlessly discussing marriage with a man who collected beautiful women the way the shore amassed seashells?

Like it's a business arrangement, she reminded herself. Nothing to get worked up over. "My lawyer wasn't able to clear her morning schedule. I trust we can involve her once we come to a suitable understanding."

Actually, she hadn't called her lawyer, who was neck-deep in a custody case for one of the women at the shelter. There was no way she could've bothered Gretchen with a proposal Lucas hadn't even agreed to yet.

"Lawyers are busy people," Lucas acknowledged and slid into the matching chair next to Cia instead of manning the larger, more imposing one behind the desk.

She set her back teeth together. What kind of reverse power tactic was that supposed to be?

He fished a leather bag from the floor and pulled a sheaf of papers from the center pocket, which he then handed to her. The receptionist silently entered with steaming coffee, filling the room with its rich, roasted smell. She passed it off and exited.

With a look of pure rapture stealing over his face, Lucas cupped the mug and inhaled, then drank deeply with a small moan. "Perfect. Do you think I could pay her to come live with me and make my coffee every morning?"

Cia snorted to clear the weird little tremor in her throat. Did he do everything with abandon, as if the simplest things could evoke such pleasure? "She'd probably do it for free. You know, if there were other benefits."

Shut up. Why did the mere presence of this man turn her stupid?

"You think?" Lucas swept Cia with a once-over. "Would you?"

"Ha. The other benefits couldn't possibly be good enough

to warrant making coffee. You're on your own." Her eyes trailed over the sheaf of papers in her hand. "What's all this?"

"A draft of a prenuptial agreement. Also, a contract laying out the terms of our marriage and divorce agreement." Lucas scrutinized her over the rim of his mug as he took a sip. He swallowed, clearly savoring the sensation of coffee sliding down his throat. "And one for the sale of Manzanares."

Taken aback, she laughed and thumbed through the papers. "No, really. What is it?"

He sat back in his chair without a word as she skimmed through the documents. He wasn't kidding—legalese covered page after page.

Now completely off balance, she cocked a brow. "Are you sleeping with your lawyer? Is that how you got all this put together so fast?"

"Sure enough," he said, easily. "Can't put nothing past you."

Great. So he'd no doubt ensured all the terms favored him. Why hadn't she had her own documents drawn up last week? She'd had plenty of time, and it threw her for a loop to be so unprepared. Business was supposed to be her niche. It was the only real skill she brought to the equation when continuing her mother's work. If passion was all it took, her mother would have single-handedly saved every woman in danger.

"Run down the highlights for me, Wheeler. What sort of lovely surprises do you have buried in here?"

It dawned on her then. He was on board. She'd talked Lucas Wheeler into marrying her. Elation flooded her stomach so hard, it cramped. *Take that, Abuelo.* Her grandfather thought he was so smart, locking up the money, and she'd figured out a way to get it after all.

"No surprises. We each retain ownership of our assets. It's all there in black and white." His phone beeped, but he ignored it in favor of giving her his full attention. "You were up front with me, and I appreciate that. No better way to start a partnership than with honesty. So I'll direct your attention to page fifteen."

He waited until she found the page, which took longer than it should have, but she had this spiky, keen awareness of him watching her, and it stiffened her fingers. "Fifteen. Got it."

"I want you to change your name to Wheeler. It's my only stipulation. And it's nonnegotiable."

"No." She spit out the word, eyes still stumbling over the lines of his unreasonable demand. "That's ridiculous. We're going to be married for a short time, in name only."

"Exactly. That means you have to do the name part."

The logic settled into her gut and needled. Hard. She couldn't do it, couldn't give up the link with her parents and declare herself tied to this man every time she gave her name. It was completely irrational. Completely old-fashioned. *Cia Wheeler.* And appalling. "I can't even hyphenate? No deal. You have to take out that stipulation."

Instead of arguing, he unfolded his long frame from the chair and held out his hand. "Come with me. I'd like to show you something."

Nothing short of a masked man with an Uzi could make her touch him. She stood without the offered hand and scouted around his pristine, well-organized office for something worth noting. "Show me what?"

"It's not here. I have to drive you."

"I don't have all day to cruise around with you, Wheeler." If his overwhelming masculinity disturbed her this much in a spacious office, how much more potent would it be in a tiny car?

"Then we should go."

Without waiting for further argument, he led her out a back entrance to a sleek, winter-white, four-door Mercedes and opened the passenger door before she could do it. To make a point, obviously, that he called the shots.

She sank into the creamy leather and fumed. Lucas Wheeler

was proving surprisingly difficult to maneuver, and a husband she couldn't run rings around had not been part of the plan. According to all the society articles she'd read, he only cared about the next gorgeous, sophisticated woman and the next party, presumably because he wasn't overly ambitious or even very bright.

Okay, the articles hadn't said that. *She'd* made presumptions, perhaps without all the facts.

He started the car and pulled out of the lot. Once on the street, he gradually sped up to a snail's pace. She sat on her hands so she couldn't fiddle with a hem. When that failed, she bit alternate cheeks and breathed in new-car smell mixed with leather conditioner and whatever Lucas wore that evoked a sharp, clean pine forest.

She couldn't stand it a second longer. "*Madre de Dios,* Wheeler. You drive like my grandfather. Are we going to get there before midnight?"

That drawn-out, dangerous smile flashed into place. "Well, now, darlin', what's your hurry? Half the fun is getting there and the pleasures to be had along the way, don't you think?"

The vibe spilling off him said they weren't talking about driving at all. The car shrank, and it had already been too small for both her and the sex machine in the driver's seat.

Slouching down, she crossed her arms over the slow burn kicking up in her abdomen. Totally against her will, she pictured Lucas doing all sorts of things excruciatingly slowly.

How did he do that? She'd have sworn her man repellant was foolproof. It had worked often enough in the past to keep her out of trouble. "No. I don't think. The fun is all in the end goal. Can't get to the next step unless you complete the one before. Taking your time holds that up."

Lucas shook his head. "No wonder you're so uptight. You don't relax enough."

"I relax, women suffer. Where are we going? And what does all this have to do with me changing my name? Which

I am not going to do, by the way, regardless of whatever it is we're going to see."

He fell quiet for a long moment, and she suspected it wasn't the last time she'd squirm with impatience until he made his move. Their whole relationship was going to be an unending chess match, and she'd left her pawns at home.

"Why don't we listen to the radio?" he said out of nowhere. "Pick a station."

"I don't want to listen to the radio." And if she kept snapping at him, he'd know exactly how far under her skin he'd gotten. She had to do better than this.

"I'll pick one, then," he said in that amiable tone designed to fool everyone into thinking he couldn't pour water out of a boot with instructions printed on the heel. Not her, though. She was catching on quick.

George Strait wailed from the high-end speakers and smothered her with a big ol' down-home layer of twangy guitars. "Are you trying to put me to sleep?"

With a fingertip, she hit the button on the radio until she found a station playing Christina Aguilera.

"Oh, much better," Lucas said sarcastically and flipped off the music to drop them into blessed silence. Then he ruined it by talking. "Forget I mentioned the radio. So we'll have a quiet household. We're here."

"We are?" Cia glanced out the window. Lucas had parked in the long, curving driveway of an impressive house on a more impressive plot of painstakingly landscaped property. The French design of the house fit the exclusive neighborhood but managed to be unique, as well. "Where is here?"

"Highland Park. More specifically, our house in Highland Park," he said.

"You picked out a house? Already? Why do we need a house? What's wrong with you moving in with me?" A house was too real, too…homey.

Worse, the two-story brick house was beautiful, with elegant stone accents and gas coach lights flanking the arched entryway. Not only did Lucas have more than a couple of working brain cells, he also had amazing taste.

"This place is available now, it's close to the office and I like it. If this fake marriage is going to work, we can't act like it's fake. Everyone would wonder why we didn't want to start our lives together someplace new."

"No one is going to wonder that." Is that what normal married people did? Why hadn't she thought longer and harder about what it might take to make everyone believe she and Lucas were in love? Maybe because she knew nothing about love, except that when it went away, it took unrecoverable pieces with it. "You're not planning on sharing a bedroom, are you?"

"You tell me. This is all for your grandfather's benefit. Is he going to come over and inspect the house to be sure this is real?"

Oh, God. He wouldn't. Would he? "No, he trusts me."

And she intended to lie right to his face. Her stomach twisted.

"Then we'll do separate bedrooms." Lucas shrugged and crinkled up the corners of his eyes with a totally different sort of dangerous smile, and this one, she had no defenses against. "Check out the house. If you hate it, we'll find another one."

Mollified, she heaved a deep breath. Lucas could be reasonable. Good to know. She'd need a huge dollop of reasonable to talk him out of the Cia Wheeler madness. *Dios,* it didn't even sound right. The syllables clacked together like a hundred cymbals flung against concrete.

She almost got the car door open before Lucas materialized at her side to open it the rest of the way. At least he had the wisdom not to try to help her out. With a steel-straight spine, she swung out of the car and followed him to the front door, which he opened with a flourish, then pocketed the key.

With its soaring ceilings and open floor plan, the house

was breathtaking. No other word would do. Her brain wasn't quick on the draw anyway with a solid mass of Lucas hot at her back as she stopped short in the marble, glass and dark wood foyer.

He skirted around her and walked into the main living area off the foyer.

Heavy dustcovers were draped over furniture, and heavier silence added to the empty atmosphere. People had lived here once and fled, leaving behind fragments of themselves in their haste. Why? And why did she want to fling off the covers and recapture some of the happiness someone had surely experienced here once upon a time?

"Well?" Lucas asked, his voice low in the stillness. "Do you want to keep looking? Or will it do?"

The quirk of his mouth said he already knew the answer. She didn't like being predictable. Especially not to him. "How did you find this place?"

He studied her, and, inexplicably, she wished he'd flash that predatory smile she hated. At least then his thoughts would be obvious and she'd easily deflect his charm. This seriousness freaked her out a little.

"Vacant properties are my specialty," he said. "Hazard of the job. The owner was willing to rent for six months, so it's a no-brainer. Would you like to see the kitchen? It's this way."

He gestured to the back of the house, but she didn't budge.

"I don't have to see the kitchen to recognize a setup. You're in commercial real estate, not residential. Why did you bring me here?"

"I'm throwing down my hand." He lifted his chin. In the dim light, his eyes glinted, opening up a whole other dimension to his appeal, and it stalled her breath. What was wrong with her? Maybe she needed to eat.

"Great," she squeaked and sucked in a lungful of air. "What's in it?"

In a move worthy of a professional magician, he twirled

his hand and produced a small black box. "Your engagement ring."

Her heart fluttered.

Romance didn't play a part in her life. Reality did. Before this moment, marrying Lucas had only been an idea, a nebulous concept invented to help them reach their individual goals. Now it was a fact.

And the sight of a man like Lucas with a ring box gripped in his strong fingers shouldn't make her throat ache because this was the one and only proposal she'd ever get.

"We haven't talked about any of this." She hadn't been expecting a ring. Or a house. She hadn't thought that far ahead. "Do you want me to pay half?"

"Nah." He waved away several thousand dollars with a flick of his hand. "Consider the ring a gift. Give it back at the end if it makes you feel better."

"It's not even noon, Wheeler. So far, you've presented me with contracts, a house and a ring. Either you already planned to ask someone else to marry you or you have a heck of a personal assistant." She crossed her arms as she again took in the fatigue around his eyes.

Oh. That's why he was tired. He'd spent the hours since she'd sprung this divorce deal on him getting all this arranged, yet he still managed to look delicious in a freshly pressed suit.

She refused to be impressed. Refused to reorganize her assumptions about the slick pretty boy standing in the middle of the house he'd picked out for them.

So he hadn't been tearing up the sheets with his lawyer all night. So he'd rearranged his appointments to bring her here. So what?

"Last night, you proposed a partnership," he said. "That means we both bring our strengths to the table, and that's what I'm doing. Fact of the matter is you need me and for more than a signature on a piece of paper. You want everyone to believe this marriage is real, but you don't seem to have any concept of how to go about it."

"Oh, and you do?" she shot back and cursed the quaver in her voice.

Of course she didn't know how to be married, for real or otherwise. How could she? Every day, she helped women leave their husbands and boyfriends, then taught them to build new, independent lives.

Every day, she reminded herself that love was for other people, for those who could figure out how to do it without glomming on to a man, expecting him to fix all those emotionally bereft places inside, like she'd done in college right after her parents' deaths.

"Yeah. I've been around my parents for thirty years. My brother was married. My grandfather is married. The name of the company isn't Wheeler Family Partners because we like the sound of it. I work with married men every day."

Somehow he'd moved back into the foyer, where she'd remained. He was close. Too close. When he reached out to sweep hair from her cheek, she jumped.

"Whoa there, darlin'. See, that's not how married people act. They touch each other. A lot." There was that killer smile, and it communicated all the scandalous images doubtlessly swimming through his head. "And, honey, they like to touch each other. You're going to have to get used to it."

Right. She unclenched her fists.

They'd have to pretend to be lovey-dovey in public, and they'd have to practice in private. But she didn't have to start this very minute.

She stepped back, away from the electricity sparking between her and this man she'd deny to her grave being attracted to. The second she gave in, it was all over. *Feelings* would start to creep in and heartbreak would follow. "The house will do. I'll split the rent with you."

With a raised eyebrow, he said, "What about the ring? You haven't even looked at it."

"As long as it's round, it's fine, too."

"I might have to get it sized. Here, try it." He flipped open the lid and plucked out a whole lot of sparkle. When he slid it on her finger, she nearly bit her tongue to keep a stupid female noise of appreciation from slipping out. The ring fit perfectly and caught the sunlight from the open front door, igniting a blaze in the center of the marble-size diamond.

"Flashy. Exactly what I would have picked out." She tilted her hand in the other direction to set off the fiery rainbow again.

"Is that your subtle way of demonstrating yet again how much you need me?" He chuckled. "Women don't pick out their own engagement rings. Men do. This one says Lucas Wheeler in big letters."

No, it said Lucas Wheeler's Woman in big letters.

For better or worse, that's what she'd asked to be for the next six months, and the ring would serve as a hefty reminder to her and everyone else. She *had* proposed a partnership; she just hadn't expected it to be fifty-fifty. Furthermore, she'd royally screwed up by not thinking through how to present a fake marriage as real to the rest of the world.

Lucas had been right there, filling in the gaps, picking up the slack and doing his part. She should embrace what he brought to the table instead of fighting him, which meant she had to go all the way.

"I'll take the contracts to my lawyer this afternoon. As is."

Cia Wheeler. It made her skin crawl.

But she was perfectly capable of maintaining her independence, no matter what else Lucas threw at her. It was only a name, and with the trust money in her bank account, the shelter her mother never had a chance to build would become a reality. That was the true link to her parents, and she'd change her name back the second the divorce was final. "When can we move in?"

Three

Cia eased into her grandfather's study, tiptoeing in deference to his bowed head and scribbling hand, but his seventy-year-old faculties hadn't dimmed in the slightest. He glanced up from the desk, waved her in and scratched out another couple of sentences on his yellow legal pad. Paper and pen, same as he'd used for decades. Benicio Allende owned one of the premier technology companies in the world, yet remained firmly entrenched in the past.

A tiny bit of guilt over the lie she was about to tell him curled her toes.

Abuelo folded his hands and regarded her with his formidable deep-set gaze. "What brings you by today?"

Of course he cut right to the purpose of her unusual visit, and she appreciated it. A dislike of extraneous decorum was the only thing they had in common. When she'd come to live with him after her parents' accident, the adjustment had been steep on both sides. Prior to that, he'd been just as much her dad's boss as her dad's father. She'd long since stopped wishing for a grandfather with mints in his pocket and a twinkly smile.

Instead, she'd gleaned everything she could from him about how to succeed.

"Hello, Abuelo. I have some news. I'm getting married." Better leave it at that. He'd ask questions to get the pertinent information.

Their stiff holiday dinners and occasional phone calls had taught her not to indulge in idle chatter, especially not about her personal life. Nothing made him more uncomfortable than the subject of his granddaughter dating.

"To whom?"

"Lucas Wheeler." Whose diamond glittered from her third finger, weighing down her hand. She'd almost forgotten the ring that morning and had had to dash back to slip it on. A happily engaged woman wouldn't even have taken it off. "Of Wheeler Family Partners."

"Fine family. Very good choice." He nodded once, and she let out a breath. He hadn't heard the rumors about Lucas and his affair with the married woman. Usually Abuelo didn't pay attention to gossip. But nothing about this fake marriage was usual.

"I'm glad you approve."

The antique desk clock ticked as Abuelo leaned back in his chair, his shock of white hair a stark contrast to black leather. "I'm surprised he didn't come with you for a proper introduction."

Lucas had insisted he should do exactly that, but she'd talked him out of it in case Abuelo didn't buy the story she and Lucas had concocted. Everything hinged on getting over this hurdle, and she needed to handle it on her own. She owed Lucas that much.

"I wanted to tell you myself first. We're getting married so quickly…I knew it could be viewed as impulsive, but I actually dated Lucas previously. When I started focusing on other things, we drifted apart. He never forgot me. We re-united by chance at an event last week, and it was as if we'd never been separated."

Dios. When she and Lucas had discussed the story, it hadn't sounded so ridiculously romantic. Since she'd never talked to Abuelo about her love life, hopefully he wouldn't clue in on the implausibility of his granddaughter being swept off her feet.

"Other things? You mean the shelter." Abuelo's brows drew into a hawklike line. He didn't like the way she'd buried her-self in her mother's passion and never missed an opportunity to harp on it, usually by telling her what her life should look like instead. "I expect you'll now focus on your husband, as a wife should."

Yeah, that was going to happen.

Abuelo was convinced a husband would make her forget all about the shelter and help her move past the loss of her par-ents. He grieved for his son and daughter-in-law by banishing them from his mind and couldn't accept that she grieved by tirelessly pursuing her mother's goal—a fully funded shelter with no danger of being closed due to lack of money.

Her grandfather refused to understand that the shelter pro-vided more lasting satisfaction than a husband ever could.

"I know what's expected of me in this marriage."

Did she ever. She had to pretend to be in love with a man who turned her brain into a sea sponge. Still, it was worth it.

"Excellent. I'm very pleased with this union. The Wheeler fortune is well established."

Translation—she'd managed to snag someone who wasn't a fortune hunter, the precise reason Abuelo hadn't tied the trust to marriage. The reminder eliminated the last trace of her guilt. If he'd shown faith in her judgment, a fake mar-riage could have been avoided.

"I'm pleased that you're pleased."

"Dulciana, I want you to be happy. I hope you understand this."

"I do." Abuelo, though fearsome at times, loved her in his way. They just had different definitions of *happy*. "I'm grateful for your guidance."

He evaluated her for a moment, his wrinkles deepening as he frowned. "I don't pretend to understand your avid interest in hands-on charity work, but perhaps after you've established your household, you may volunteer a few hours a week. If your husband is supportive."

She almost laughed. "Lucas and I have already come to an agreement about that. Thanks, though, for the suggestion. By the way, we're going to have a small civil ceremony with no guests. It's what we both want."

"You're not marrying in the church?"

The sting in his tone hit its mark with whipping force. She'd known this part couldn't be avoided but had left it for last on purpose. "Lucas is Protestant."

And divorce was not easily navigated after a Catholic ceremony. The plan was sticky enough without adding to it.

"Sit," he commanded, and with a sigh, she settled into the creaky leather chair opposite the desk.

Now she was in for it—Abuelo would have to be convinced she'd made these decisions wisely. In his mind, she was clearly still a seventeen-year-old orphan in need of protection from the big, bad world. She put her game face on and waded into battle with her hardheaded grandfather, determined to win his approval.

After all, everything she knew about holding her ground she'd learned from him.

Four days, two phone calls and one trip to notarize the contracts and apply for a marriage license later, Lucas leaned on the doorjamb of Matthew's old house—correction, his and

Cia's house, for now anyway—and watched Cia pull into the driveway. In a red Porsche.

What an excellent distraction from the text message his brother had just sent—We lost Schumacher Industrial. Lucas appreciated the omission of "thanks to you."

Matthew never passed around blame, which of course heightened Lucas's guilt. If Wheeler Family Partners folded, he'd have destroyed the only thing his brother had left.

As Cia leaped out of the car, he hooked a thumb in the pocket of his cargos and whistled. "That's a mighty fine point-A-to-point-B ride, darlin'. Lots of starving children in Africa could be fed with those dollars."

"Don't trip over your jaw, Wheeler," she called and slammed the door, swinging her dark ponytail in an arc. "My grandfather gave me this car when I graduated from college, and I have to drive something."

"Doesn't suck that it goes zero to sixty in four-point-two seconds, either. Right, my always-in-a-hurry fiancée?" His grin widened as she stepped up on the porch, glare firmly in place. "Come on, honey. Lighten up. The next six months are going to be long and tedious if you don't."

"The next six months are going to be long and tedious no matter what. My grandfather is giving us a villa in Mallorca as a wedding present. A *villa,* Wheeler. What do I say to that? 'No, thanks, we'd prefer china,'" she mimicked in a high voice and wobbled her head. That dark ponytail flipped over her shoulder.

The times he'd been around her previously, she'd always had her hair down. And had been wearing some nondescript outfit.

Today, in honor of moving day no doubt, she'd pulled on a hot-pink T-shirt and jeans. Both hugged her very nice curves, and the ponytail revealed an intriguing expanse of neck, which might be the only vulnerable place on Cia's body.

Every day should be moving day.

"Tell your grandfather to make a donation, like I told my parents. How come my family has to follow the rules but yours doesn't?"

"I did. You try telling my grandfather what to do. *Es imposible.*" She threw up her hands, and he bit back a two-bulldozers-one-hole comment, which she would not have appreciated and wouldn't have heard anyway because she rushed on. "He's thrilled to pieces about me marrying you, God knows why, and bought the reunion story, hook, line and sinker."

"Hey now," Lucas protested. "I'm an upstanding member of the community and come from a long line of well-respected businessmen. Why wouldn't he be thrilled?"

"Because you're—" she flipped a hand in his direction, and her engagement ring flashed "—you. Falling in and out of bimbos' beds with alarming frequency and entirely too cocky for your own good. Are we going inside? I'd like to put the house in some kind of order."

Enough was enough. He tolerated slurs—some deserved, some not—from a lot of people. Either way, his wife wasn't going to be one of them.

"Honey?" He squashed the urge to reach out and lift her chin. Determined to get her to meet him halfway, he instead waited until she looked at him. "Listen up. What you see is what you get. I'm not going to apologize for rubbing you the wrong way. I like women, and I won't apologize for that, either. But I haven't dated anyone since Lana, and you're pushing my considerable patience to the limit if you're suggesting I'd sleep with another woman while my ring is on your finger. Even if the ring is for show."

A slight breeze separated a few strands of hair from the rest of her ponytail as she stared up at him, frozen, with a hint of confusion flitting across her face. "No. I didn't mean that. It was, uh… I'm sorry. Don't be mad. I'll keep my big mouth shut from now on."

He laughed. "Darlin', I don't get mad. I get even."

With that, he swept her off her feet and carried her over the threshold. She weighed less than cotton candy, and her skin was fresh with the scent of coconut and lime. Did she smell like that all the time or only on moving day?

Her curled fist whacked him in the shoulder, but he ignored it, too entranced by the feel of previously undiscovered soft spots hidden amid all her hard edges.

"What is this?" she sputtered. "Some caveman show of dominance?"

Gently, he set down the bundle of bristling woman on the marble floor in the foyer.

"Neighbors were watching," he said, deadpan.

They hadn't been. Matthew had carried Amber over the threshold and had told the story a bunch of times about nicking the door frame when he whacked it with his new bride's heel.

Lucas had always envisioned doing that with his way, way, way in the future wife, too—minus the door frame whacking—and wasn't about to let the Queen of Contrary tell him no. Even if they weren't technically married yet. Close enough, and it was practice for the eventual real deal, where his wife would gaze at him adoringly as he carried her.

He couldn't get a clear picture of this fictitious future wife. In his imagination, Cia reappeared in his arms instead.

"We have an agreement." She jammed her hands down onto her hips. "No division of property. No messiness. And *no* physical relationship. What happened to that?"

He smirked. "That wasn't even close to physical, darlin'. Now, if I was to do this—" he snaked an arm around her waist and hauled her up against him, fitting her into the niches of his body "—I'd be getting warmer."

She wiggled a little in protest and managed to slide right into a spot that stabbed a hot poker through his groin. He sucked in a cleansing breath.

This was *Cia,* the most beautiful and least arousing female he'd ever met. Why did his skin feel as if it was about to combust? "That's right. Snuggle right in, honey. Now that's so close to physical, it's scorching hot."

"What are you doing, Wheeler?" She choked on the last syllable as he leaned in, a hairbreadth from tasting that high-speed mouth, and trailed a finger down her tight jaw.

"Practicing."

If he moved one tiny neck muscle the right way, they'd be kissing. Soon, this firecracker in his arms would be Mrs. Lucas Wheeler, and he hadn't kissed her once. Maybe he should. Might shut her up for a minute.

"Practicing for what?"

"To be a happy couple. My parents invited us over for dinner tonight. Engagement celebration." Instantly she stopped wiggling, and the light hit her upturned face and her wide, frightened eyes. "Well, I'll be hog-tied and spoon-fed to vultures for breakfast. Your eyes are blue. Not brown."

"My grandparents came from northern Spain. It's not that unusual."

"A man should know the color of his wife's eyes. Marriage 101." Disconcerted, he released her. He had to get her scent out of his nose.

He shoved a hand through his hair, but it didn't release a bit of the sudden pressure against his skull.

He'd wanted to kiss her. It had taken a whole lot of willpower not to. What had he gotten himself into?

He barely knew her, knew nothing about how to handle her, nothing about her past or even her present. He had to learn. Fast.

The Manzanares contract represented more than a vital shot in the arm for his livelihood. It was a chance to fix his problems on his own, without his big brother's help, and prove to everyone that Lucas Wheeler wasn't the screw-up womanizer people assumed.

"What else don't I know?" he asked.

"That I have to work tonight. I can't go to your parents' for dinner. You have to check with me about this kind of stuff."

Yeah. He should have. It hadn't occurred to him. Most women of his acquaintance would have stood up the president in order to have dinner with his parents. He'd just never invited any of them. "Call in. Someone else can cover it. This is important to my mother."

"The shelter is important to me. Someone else has been covering my responsibilities all week." Her hands clenched and went rigid by her sides. "It's not like I'm canceling a round of golf with a potential client, Wheeler."

Golf. Yeah. His workday consisted of eye-crossing, closed-door sessions with Matthew, poring over his brother's newest strategies to improve business. "What is it like, then? Tell me."

"The women who come to the shelter are terrified their husbands or boyfriends will find them, even though we go to extreme lengths to keep the location secret. Their kids have been uprooted, jammed into a crowded, foreign new home and have lost a father, all at the same time. They're desperate for someone they know and trust. Me."

Bright, shiny moisture gathered in the pockets of her eyes as she spoke, and that caught him in the throat as much as her heartfelt speech. No one could fake that kind of passion for a job. Or anything else. "Dinner tomorrow night, then."

Mama would have to understand. God Almighty, what a balancing act. The ripples were starting already, and it was going to be hell to undo the effects after the divorce.

He had to believe it would be worth it. He had to believe he could somehow ensure his family didn't get attached to Cia without vilifying her in the process. He needed a nice, stable wife to combat the Lana Effect nearly as much as he needed Manzanares.

She nodded, and a tear broke loose to spill down her cheek. "Thanks."

All of a sudden, he felt strangely honored to be part of something so meaningful to her. Sure, his own stake meant a lot, too, but it was nice that his investment in this fake marriage would benefit others.

"Come on." He slung an arm around her slim shoulders. Such a small frame to hold so much inside. "Better. You didn't even flinch that time."

"I'm trying." As if to prove it, she didn't shrug off his arm.

"We'll get there."

Legs bumping, he guided her toward the kitchen, where he'd left every single box intact because God forbid he accidentally put the blender in the wrong spot.

Most of Amber's touches had been removed, thrown haphazardly into the trash by a blank-faced Matthew, but a few remained, like the empty fruit bowl his sister-in-law had picked up at the farmers' market.

Must have missed that one. During those weeks following the funeral, even he had been numb over Amber's sudden death, and neither he nor Matthew had put a whole lot of effort into clearing the house.

Maybe, in some ways, his marriage to Cia would be a lot easier than one built on the promise of forever. At least he knew ahead of time it was ending and there would be no emotional investment to reconcile.

"Look how far we've come already," he told her. "You're not going to make cracks about my past relationships, and I'm not going to make plans for dinner without checking first. The rest will be a snap. You just have to pretend you love me as much as you love being a crusader. Easy, right?"

She snorted and some color returned to her cheeks.

Good. Hell's bells, was she ever a difficult woman, but without him, she'd be lost. She had no idea how to fake a relationship. Her fire and compassion could only go so far, though he liked both more than he would have thought. If she ditched that prickly pear personality, she'd be something else. Thank the good Lord she hadn't.

Otherwise, he'd be chomping at the bit to break the no-physical-relationship rule and that would be plain stupid. Like kissing her would have been stupid.

No complications. That was the best way to ensure he put Wheeler Family Partners back on the map. He and Cia were business partners, and her proposal challenged him to be something he'd never been before—the hero. She deserved his undivided attention to this deal.

But he had to admit he liked that she wasn't all that comfortable having a man's hands on her. Maybe he had some caveman in him after all.

Cia spent a few hours arranging the kitchen but had to get to the shelter before finishing. Okay, so she took off earlier than planned because there was too much Lucas in the house.

How could she sleep there tonight? Or the next night or the next?

This was it, the real thing.

She'd taken her bedroom furniture, clothes and a few other necessary items, then locked up her condo. She and Lucas now lived together. They'd attend Mr. and Mrs. Wheeler's engagement dinner tomorrow night, and a blink after making the man's acquaintance, she'd marry Lucas at the courthouse Monday afternoon.

Cia Wheeler. It wasn't as if Lucas had made forty-seven other unreasonable demands. It was petty to keep being freaked about it.

So she spent a lot of her shift trying to get used to the name, practicing it aloud and writing it out several hundred times while she manned the check-in desk.

Dios, she'd turned into a love-struck teenager, covering an entire blank page with loopy script. *Mrs. Lucas Wheeler.*

Cia Wheeler. Dulciana Alejandra de Coronado y Allende Wheeler. Like her full name hadn't already been pretentious enough. Well, she wouldn't be writing that anywhere except on the marriage certificate.

The evening vaporized, and the next set of volunteers arrived. Cia took her time saying goodbye to everyone and checked on Pamela Gonzalez twice to be sure she was getting along okay as her broken arm healed.

A couple of weeks ago, Cia had taken the E.R. nurse's call and met Pamela at the hospital to counsel her on options; then she'd driven Pamela to the shelter personally.

Victims often arrived still bloodstained and broken, but Cia considered it a win to get them to a safe place they likely wouldn't have known about without her assistance. It wasn't as if the shelter could advertise an address or every abuser would be at the door, howling for his woman to be returned.

Pamela smiled and shooed Cia out of the room, insisting she liked her three roommates and would be fine. With nothing left to do, Cia headed for the new house she shared with her soon-to-be husband, braced for whatever he tossed out this time.

She found Lucas's bedroom door shut as she passed the master suite on the way to her smaller bedroom.

She let out a rush of pent-up air. A glorious, blessed reprieve from "practicing" and that smile and those broad shoulders, which filled a T-shirt as if Lucas had those custom-made along with his suits. A reprieve by design or by default she didn't know, and she didn't care. Gratefully, she sank into bed and slept until morning.

By the time she emerged from her room, Lucas was already gone. She ate a quick breakfast in the quiet kitchen someone had lovingly appointed with warm colors, top-of-the-line appliances and rich tile.

The house came equipped with a central music hub tied to the entertainment system in the living room, and after a few minutes of poking at the touch-screen remote, she blasted an electronica number through the speakers. Then she went to work unpacking the remainder of her boxes.

Sometime later, Lucas found her sitting on the floor in the living room, straightening books. She hit the volume on the remote, painfully aware that compromise and consideration, the components of a shared life, were now her highest priority.

"You're up," he said and flopped onto the couch. His hair was damp, turning the sunny blond to a deep gold, and he wore what she assumed were his workout clothes, shorts and a Southern Methodist University football T-shirt. "I didn't know how late you'd sleep. I tried to be quiet. Did I wake you?"

"You didn't. I always sleep in when I work the evening shift at the shelter. I hope I didn't make too much noise when I came in."

"Nah." He shrugged. "We'll learn each other's schedules soon enough I guess."

"About that."

She rose, shook the cramps out of her knees—how long had she been sitting there?—and crossed to the matching leather couch at a right angle to the one cradling entirely too much of Lucas's long, tanned and well-toned legs. "I appreciate the effort you put into making all this possible. I want to do my part, so I found a questionnaire online that the immigration office uses to validate green card marriages. Here's a copy for you, to help us learn more about each other." He was staring at her as if she'd turned into a bug splattered on his windshield. "You know, so we can make everyone believe we're in love."

"That's how you plan to pretend we're a real couple? Memorize the brand of shaving cream I use?"

"It's good enough for the immigration department," she countered. "There are lots of other questions in here besides brand names. Like, which side of the bed does your spouse sleep on? Where did you meet? You're the one who pointed out I haven't got a clue how to be married. This is my contribution. How did you think we would go about it?"

His eyes roamed over the list and narrowed. "A long conversation over dinner, along with a good bottle of wine. The way people do when they're dating."

"We're not dating, Wheeler." *Dating.* Something else she had no idea how to do. If she'd had a normal high school experience, maybe that wouldn't be the case. "And we don't have that kind of time. Your parents' party is tonight."

"Yeah, but they're not going to ask questions like which side of the bed you sleep on."

"No. They'll ask questions like how we met." She stabbed the paper. "Or what made us decide to get married so quickly. Or where we plan to go on our honeymoon. Look at the questionnaire. It's all there."

"This is too much like school," he grumbled and swept a lock of hair off his forehead. "Is there going to be a written exam with an essay question? What happens if I don't pass?"

"My grandfather gets suspicious. Then I don't get my money. Women don't get a place to escape from the evil they live with. You don't get the Manzanares contract." She rattled the printed pages. "Pick a question."

"Can I at least take a shower before spilling my guts?"

"Only if you answer number eighteen."

He glanced at the paper and stood, clearly about to scram as soon as he recited the response. "'What do the two of you have in common?'" Eyebrows raised, he met her gaze. Then he sat back down. "This is going to take hours."

"I tried to tell you."

For the rest of the day, in between Lucas's shower, lunch, grocery shopping and an unfinished argument over what Cia proposed to wear to dinner, they shot questions back and forth. He even followed her to her room, refusing to give her a minute alone.

Exhausted, Cia dropped onto her bed and flung a hand over her eyes. "This is a disaster."

Lucas rooted around in her closet, looking for an unfrumpy dress. So far, he'd discarded her three best dresses from Macy's, which he refused to acknowledge were practical, and was working up to insulting the more casual ones in the back.

"I agree. Your wardrobe is a cardigan away from an episode of Grandmas Gone Mild." Lucas emerged from her closet, shaking his head. "We gotta fix that."

"Nowhere in our agreement did it say I was required to dress like a bimbo. You are not allowed to buy me clothes. Period." Knowing him, he'd burn her old outfits, and then what would she wear to the shelter? BCBG and Prada to work with poverty-stricken women? "That's not the disaster."

"You dressing like something other than a matronly librarian is for my benefit, not yours. What could possibly be more of a disaster than your closet?"

It was disconcerting to have that much Lucas in her bedroom, amid her familiar mission-style furniture, which was decorating an unfamiliar house. An unfamiliar house they would share for a long six months. "Do you realize we have nothing in common other than both being born in Texas and both holding a business degree from SMU?"

He leaned his jean-clad rear on her dresser, and *Dios en las alturas,* the things acid-washed denim did to his thighs. *Not noticing,* she chanted silently. *Not noticing at all.*

But therein lay the problem. It was impossible not to notice Lucas. He lit up the room—a golden searchlight stabbing the black sky, drawing her eye and piquing her curiosity.

"What about bourbon?" he asked. "You drink that."

"Three things in common, then. *Three.* Why didn't I look for someone who at least knows how to spell hip-hop?"

His nose wrinkled. "Because. That's not important. Marriages aren't built on what you have in common. It's about not being able to live without each other."

First clothes. Then declarations à la Romeo and Juliet. "Are you sure you're not gay?"

"Would you like to come over here and test me? Now, darlin', that's the kind of exam I can get on board with." His electric gaze traveled over her body sprawled out on the bed, and she resisted the intense urge to dive under the covers. To hide from that sexy grin.

"Save it for tonight, Wheeler. Go away so I can get dressed."

"No can do. You've maligned my orientation, and I'm not having it." He advanced on her, and a dangerous edge sprang into his expression. "There must be a suitable way to convince you. Shall I make your ears bleed with a range of baseball statistics? Rattle off a bunch of technical specs for the home theater system in the media room down the hall? Hmm. No, none of that stuff is specific to straight men. Only one way to go on this one."

In an effortless move, he tumbled onto the bed, wrapped her up in his arms and rolled, tangling their legs and binding her to his hard body. Heat engulfed her, and that unique, woodsy Lucas scent swirled through her head in a drugging vortex.

When his lips grazed the hollow beneath her ear, she gasped for air as the world ignited around her.

Lucas's fingers threaded through her hair, and his mouth burned down her throat. The impressive evidence of his orientation pressed against her thigh, and she went liquid.

The plan to ignore her feminine parts for the next six months melted faster than ice in the blazing sun.

This wasn't supposed to be happening, this flood of need for a man who did this for sport. She was smarter than that.

He hadn't even kissed her yet.

"Stop," she choked out before surrender became inevitable.

No doubt he could make her body sing like a soprano with little effort. But intimacy at that level was never going to happen for her. Not with anybody. She'd learned her lesson the hard way in college, and it still stung.

He took one look at her face and swore, then rolled away to stare at the ceiling. "I'm sorry. That was juvenile, even for me. Please, let's pretend I'm not such a jerk."

She jumped off the bed and backed away from the slightly rumpled and wholly inviting male lying in it. "It's not a big deal. I know you were only messing around."

"It is a big deal. You're skittish enough already." He glanced up at her, and darkness dawned in his eyes. "Oh, man, I'm slow, I'll admit, but I shouldn't be *that* slow. Some guy beat up on you, didn't he? That's why you're so passionate about the shelter."

"What? No way. I teach self-defense. Any creep who laid a hand on me would find his balls in his back pocket. If I was in a good enough mood to return them."

"Then why are you so scared of men touching you?"

"I'm not scared of men touching me." *Just you.* History proved she couldn't trust herself, and she didn't plan to test it.

She shrugged and prayed her expression conveyed boredom or nonchalance or anything other than what she was feeling. "I'm just not interested in you that way. And that little interlude was four exits past practicing. We'll never have a public occasion to be lying in bed together."

Her tone could have frosted glass, and he didn't overlook it. In his typical fashion, he grinned and said, "I might have missed the exit for practicing, but the one I took had some great scenery. Meet me downstairs at six?"

She tried to be irritated but couldn't. He'd apologized and put them back on even ground effortlessly. No point in sulking about it. "I'll be downstairs at six. I'll expect you about ten after."

Chuckling, he left and shut the door behind him, sucking

all the vibrancy out of the room. She took a not-so-hot shower and washed her hair twice but couldn't erase the feeling of Lucas's fingers laced through it. The towel scraped across her still-sensitized flesh, and she cursed. She couldn't give him any more openings. It was too hard to fake a nonreaction.

In deference to Lucas's parents, she spent an extra couple of minutes on her hair and makeup. Lucas would likely complain about her lack of style regardless, so it certainly wasn't for his sake. The less she encouraged the trigger on his libido, the better.

With a small sigh, she twisted Lucas's diamond ring onto her finger, the only jewelry a man had ever bought her, and pretended she hated it.

Four

After firing off at least half a dozen emails and scheduling a couple of walk-throughs for early Monday afternoon, Lucas descended the hardwood and wrought-iron stairs at six sharp. Dinner was important to Mama, which meant being on time, plus he'd already done enough to provoke Cia today. Though she should be apologizing to him for the solid fifteen minutes it had taken to scrub the coconut and lime from his skin.

Why did that combination linger, like a big, fruity, tropical tattoo etched into his brain? Couldn't she wear plain old Chanel like normal women? Then the slight hard-on he'd endured since being in Cia's bed, her luscious little body twisted around his, would be easy to dismiss. Easy, because a blatant, calculated turn-on he understood.

This, he didn't.

He shouldn't be attracted to her. Keeping his hands to himself should be easy. Besides, he scared the mess out of her every time he touched her. That was reason enough to back off, and there were plenty more reasons where that one came from. He'd have to try harder to remember them.

Cia had beaten him to the living room, where she paced around the sofa in a busy circle. The demons drove her relentlessly tonight. There must be a way to still them for a little while.

"Ready?" he asked, and caught her hand to slow her down. It was shaking. "Hey. It's just dinner with some old people. It's not like barging into a birthday party and proposing to a man you've never met."

"My hands were shaking then, too." She actually cracked a tiny smile. "It's not just dinner. It's a performance. Our first one, and we have to get it right. There's no backup parachute on this ride."

"That's where you're wrong, darlin'. I always have a backup parachute in my wallet."

"Only you could twist an innocent comment into an innuendo." Her eyes flashed deep blue with an unexpected hint of humor. How had he ever thought they were brown?

"If you don't like it, stop giving me ammo."

Her bottom lip poked out in mock annoyance, but he could see she was fighting a laugh. "You really are juvenile half the time, aren't you?"

And there she was, back in the fray. *Good.* Those shadows flitting through her eyes needed to go. Permanently. He'd enjoy helping that happen.

"Half the time? Nah. I give it my all 24/7." He winked and kissed her now-steady hand. A hand heavy with her engagement ring. Why did that flash on her finger please him so much? "But you're not nervous about dinner anymore, so mission accomplished. Before we go, can we find you some matching earrings?"

Fingers flew to her ears. "What? How did that happen?"

"Slow down once in a while maybe. Unless of course you

want my parents to think we rolled straight out of bed and got dressed in a big hurry."

She made a face and went back upstairs. The plain black dress she wore, the same one from the other night, did her figure no favors. Of course, only someone who had recently pressed up against every inch of those hidden curves would know they were there.

He groaned. All night long he'd be thinking about peeling off that dress. Which, on second thought, might not be bad. If she was his real fiancée, he'd be anticipating getting her undressed *and* the other choice activities to follow. No harm in visualizing both, to up the authenticity factor.

Imagining Cia naked was definitely not a chore.

When she returned, he tucked her against his side and herded her toward the garage before she could bolt. Once he'd settled her into the passenger seat of his car, he slid into the driver's seat and backed out.

Spring had fully sprung, stretching out the daylight, and the Bradford pears burst with white blooms, turning the trees into giant Q-tips. Likely Cia had no interest in discussing the weather, the Texas Rangers or the Dow, and he refused to sit in silence.

"You know, I've been curious." He glanced at the tight clamp of her jaw. Nerves. She needed a big-time distraction. "So you're not personally a victim of abuse, but something had to light that fire under you. What was it?"

"My aunt." She shut her eyes for a blink and bounced her knee. Repeatedly. "The time she showed up at our house with a two-inch-long split down her cheek is burned into my brain. I was six and the ghastly sight of raw flesh…"

With a shudder, she went on, "She needed stitches but refused to go to the emergency room because they have to file a report if they suspect abuse. She didn't want her husband to be arrested. So my mom fixed her up with Neosporin and

Band-Aids and tried to talk some sense into her. Leave that SOB, she says. You deserve better."

What a thing for a kid to witness. His sharpest memory from that age was scaring the maid with geckos. "She didn't listen, did she?"

"No." Cia stared out the window at the passing neighborhood.

When he looked at a house or a structure, he assessed the architectural details, evaluated the location and estimated the resale value. What did she see—the pain and cruelty the people inside its walls were capable of? "What happened?"

"He knocked her down, and she hit her head. After a two-month coma, they finally pulled the plug." Her voice cracked. "He claimed it was an accident, but fortunately the judge didn't see it that way. My mom was devastated. She poured all her grief into volunteer work at a shelter, determined to save as many other women as she could."

"So you're following in your mom's footsteps?"

"Much more than that. I went with her. For years, I watched these shattered women gain the skills and the emotional stability to break free of a monstrous cycle. That's an amazing thing, to know you helped someone get there. My mom was dedicated to it, and now she's gone." The bleak proclamation stole his attention from the road, and the staccato tap of her fingernail against the door kept it. "I have to make sure what happened to my aunt doesn't happen to anyone else. Earlier, you said marriage is about not being able to live without someone. I've seen the dark side of that, where women can't leave their abusers for all sorts of emotional reasons, and it gives me nightmares."

Oh, man. The shadows inside her solidified.

No wonder she couldn't be still, with all that going on inside. His chest pinched. She'd been surrounded by misery for far too long. No one had taken the time to teach her how to have fun. How to ditch the clouds for a while and play in the sun.

Wheeler to the rescue. "Next time you have a nightmare, you feel free to crawl in bed with me."

Her dark blue eyes fixed on him for a moment. "I'll keep that in mind. I'd prefer never to be dependent on a man in the first place, which is why I'll never get married."

"Yet that looks suspiciously like an engagement ring on your left hand, darlin'."

She rolled her eyes. "Married for real, I mean. Fake marriages are different."

"Marriage isn't about creating a dependency between two people, you know. It can be about much more."

Which meant much more to lose. Like what happened to Matthew, who'd been happy with Amber, goofy in love. They'd had all these plans. Then it was gone. Poof.

Some days, Lucas didn't know how Matthew held it together, which was reason enough to keep a relationship simple. Fun, yes. Emotional and heavy? No.

Lucas had done Matthew a favor by taking over his monument of a house, not that his brother would agree. If Matthew had his way, he'd mope around in that shrine forever. Cia had already begun dissolving Amber's ghost, exactly as Lucas had hoped.

"Looks suspiciously like a bare finger on your left hand, Wheeler. You had an affair with a married woman. Sounds like you deliberately avoid eligible women."

At what point had this conversation turned into an examination of the Lucas Wheeler Philosophy of Marriage? He hadn't realized he had one until now.

"Marrying you, aren't I?" he muttered. Lana had been an eligible woman, at least in his mind.

"Boy, *that* proves your point. I'm the woman who made you agree to divorce me before we got near an altar," she said sweetly and then jabbed the needle in further. "Gotta wonder what *your* hang-up is about marriage."

"Nagging wife with a sharp tongue would be hang-up number one," he said. "I'll get married one day. I haven't found the right woman yet."

"Not for lack of trying. What was wrong with all of your previous candidates?"

"Too needy," he said, and Cia chortled.

He should have blown off the question, or at least picked something less cliché. But cliché or not, that's what had made Lana so disappointing—she'd been the opposite of clingy and suffocating. For once, he'd envisioned a future with a woman. Instead, she'd been lying.

Had he seen the signs but chosen to ignore them?

"Exactly," she said. "Needy women depend on a man to fill holes inside."

"Who are you, Freud?"

"Business major, psych minor. I don't have any holes. Guess I must be the perfect date, then, huh, Wheeler?" She elbowed his ribs and drew a smile from him.

"Can't argue with that."

Now he understood her persistent prickliness toward men. Understood it, but didn't accept it.

Not all men were violent losers bent on dominating someone weaker. Some men appreciated a strong, independent woman. Some men might relish the challenge of a woman who went out of her way to make it clear how not interested she was five seconds after melting into a hot mess in a guy's arms.

The stronger she was, the harder she'd fall, and he could think of nothing better than rising to the challenge of catching her. Cia wasn't scared like he'd assumed, but she nursed some serious hang-ups about marriage *and* men.

Nothing about this marriage was real. None of it counted.

They had the ultimate no-strings-attached arrangement, and he knew the perfect remedy for chasing away those shadows—

not-real-doesn't-count sex with her new husband. Nothing emotional to trip over later, just lots of fun. They both knew where their relationship was going. There was no danger of Cia becoming dependent on him since he wasn't going to be around after six months and she presented no danger to his family's business.

Everyone won.

Instead of only visualizing Cia out of that boring dress, he'd seduce her out of it. And out of her hang-ups. A lot rode on successfully scamming everyone. What better way to make everyone think they were a real couple than to be one?

Temporarily, of course.

Lucas's parents lived at the other end of Highland Park, in a stately colonial two-story edging a large side lot bursting with tulips, hyacinth and sage. A silver-haired older version of Lucas answered the door at the Wheelers' house, giving Cia an excellent glimpse of how Lucas might age. She hadn't met Mr. Wheeler at the birthday party.

"Hi, I'm Andy," Mr. Wheeler said and swung the door wide.

Lucas shook his dad's hand and then ushered Cia into the Wheelers' foyer with a palm at the small of her back. The casual but reassuring touch warmed her spine, serving as a reminder that they were in this together.

Through sheer providence, she'd gained a real partner, one who didn't hesitate to solve problems she didn't know existed. One who calmed her and who paid enough attention to notice she wore different earrings. She'd never expected, never dreamed, she'd need or want any of that when concocting this scheme.

Thanks to Lucas everything was on track, and soon they could get on with their separate lives. Or as separate as possible while living under the same roof.

Lucas introduced Cia to his brother, Matthew, and Mrs.

Wheeler steered everyone into the plush living area off the main foyer.

"Cia, I'm happy to have you here. Please, call me Fran. Have a seat." Fran motioned to the cushion next to her on the beige couch, and Cia complied by easing onto it. "I must tell you, I'm quite surprised to learn you and Lucas renewed a previous relationship at my birthday party. I don't recall the two of you dating the first time."

"I don't tell you everything, Mama," Lucas interrupted, proceeding to wedge in next to Cia on the couch, thigh to thigh, his heavy arm drawing her against his torso. "You should thank me."

Fran shot her son a glance, which couldn't be interpreted as anything other than a warning, while Cia scrambled to respond.

Her entire body blipped into high alert. She stiffened and had to force each individual muscle in her back to relax, allowing her to sag against Lucas's sky-blue button-down shirt as if they snuggled on the couch five times a day. "It was a while back. A couple of years."

Matthew Wheeler, the less beautiful, less blond and less vibrant brother, cleared his throat from his position near the fireplace. "Lucas said four or five years ago."

Cia's heart fell off a cliff. Such a stupid, obvious thing to miss when they'd discussed it. Why hadn't Lucas mentioned he'd put a time frame to their fictitious previous relationship?

"Uh…well, it might have been four years," Cia mumbled. In a flash of inspiration, she told mostly the truth. "I was still pretty messed up about my parents. All through college. I barely remember dating Lucas."

His lips found her hairline and pressed against it in a simple kiss. An act of wordless sympathy but with the full force of Lucas behind those lips, it singed her skin, drawing heat into her cheeks, enflaming them. She was very aware of his

fingertips trailing absently along her bare arm and very aware
an engaged man had every reason to do it.

Except he'd never done it to her before and the little sparks
his fingers generated panged through her abdomen.

"Oh, no, of course," Fran said. "I'm so sorry to bring up
bad memories. Let's talk about something fun. Tell me about
your wedding dress."

In a desperate attempt to reorient, Cia zeroed in on Fran's
animated face. Lucas had not inherited his magnetism from
his father, as she'd assumed, but from his mother. They shared
a charisma that made it impossible to look away.

Lucas groaned, "Mama. That's not fun—that's worse than
water torture. Daddy and Matthew don't want to hear about
a dress. I don't even want to hear about that."

"Well, forgive me for trying to get to know my new daughter," Fran scolded and smiled at Cia conspiratorially. "I love
my sons, but sometimes just because the good Lord said I
have to. You I can love because I want to. The daughter of
my heart instead of my blood. We'll have lunch next week
and leave the party poopers at home, won't we?"

Cia nodded because her throat seized up and speaking
wasn't an option.

Fran already thought of her as a daughter.

Never had she envisioned them liking each other or that
Lucas's mother might want to become family by choice instead of only by law. The women at the shelter described
their husbands' mothers as difficult, interfering. Quick to
take their sons' sides. She'd assumed all new wives struggled
to coexist. *Must have horrible mother* should have been on
her criteria list.

And as long as she was redoing the list, *Zero sex appeal*
was numero uno.

"Isn't it time for dinner?" Lucas said brightly, and everyone's gaze slid off her as Fran agreed.

The yeasty scent of baked bread had permeated the air a

few minutes ago and must have jump-started Lucas's appetite. She smiled at him, grateful for the diversion, and took a minute to settle her stomach.

Andy and Matthew followed Fran's lead into the dining room adjacent to the living area, where a middle-aged woman in a black-and-white uniform bustled around the twelve-seat formal dining table. A whole roasted chicken held court in the center, flanked by white serving dishes containing more wonderful food.

Lucas didn't move. He should move. Plenty of couch on the other side of his thigh.

"Be there in a minute," he called to his family and took Cia's hand in his, casually running a thumb over her knuckles. "You okay? You don't have to have lunch with my mother. She means well, but she can be overbearing."

"No." She shook her head, barely able to form words around the sudden pounding of her pulse. "Your mother is lovely. I'm…well—we're lying to her. To your whole family. Lying to my grandfather is one thing because he's the one who came up with those ridiculous trust provisions. But this…"

"Is necessary," he finished for her. "It would be weird if I never introduced you to my parents. For now it's important to play it like a real couple. I'll handle them later. Make something up."

He didn't understand. Because he'd had a mother his whole life.

"More lies. It's clear you're all close. How many other grown sons go to their mother's birthday party and then to dinner at her house in the same week?" Cia vaulted off the couch, and Lucas rose a split second later. "I'm sorry I put you in this position. How do we do this? How do I go in there and eat dinner like we're a happy, desperately in love couple?"

"Well, when I'm in an impossible situation, and I have no idea how to do it, I think to myself, 'What would Scooby do?'"

In spite of the ache behind her eyes, a shuddery laugh

slipped out. A laugh, when she could hardly breathe around the fierce longing swimming through her heart to belong to such a family unit for real.

"Scooby would eat."

"Yep." Lucas flashed an approval-laden smile. "So here's a crazy idea. Don't take this so seriously. Let's have fun tonight. Eat a good meal with some people I happen to be related to. Once it's over, you'll be one step closer to your money and I'll be one step closer to Manzanares, which will make both of us happy. Voilà. Now we're a happy couple. Okay?"

"We're still lying to them."

"I told my parents we're engaged to be married, and that's true."

"But there's an assumption there about us—"

He cut her off with a grunt. "Stop being so black-and-white. If anyone asks, don't lie. Change the subject. My parents are waiting on us to eat dinner. You've got to figure it out."

She took a deep breath. One dinner. One short ceremony. Then it would be over. "I'm working on it."

"Maybe you need something else to think about during dinner."

In a completely natural move, Lucas curved her into his arms, giving her plenty of time to see him coming. Plenty of time to anticipate. The crackle in the air and the intent in his eyes told her precisely what he'd give her to think about.

And still, when he kissed her, the contact of Lucas's mouth against hers swept shock waves down her throat, into her abdomen, spreading with long, liquid pulls.

She'd been kissed before. She had. Not like this, by a master who transformed the innocent touching of mouths into a carnal slide toward the depths of sinful pleasure.

He cupped her jaw with a feathery caress. When her knees buckled, he squeezed her tighter against him and deepened the kiss slowly, sending the burn of a thousand torches down the length of her body.

Her brain drained out through her soles to puddle on the Wheelers' handmade rug.

Then it was over. He drew his head back a bit, and she nearly lost her balance as she took in the dark hunger darting through his expression.

He murmured, "Now, darlin'. You think about how we'll finish that later on. I know I will be."

Later?

Lucas tugged at their clasped hands, and she followed him on rubbery legs into the dining room, still raw from being kissed breathless. Raw and confused.

It didn't mean anything. It couldn't mean anything. That kiss had been window dressing. It had been a diversion to get her to lay off. She wasn't stupid. Lucas had a crackerjack gift for distraction when necessary, and this had been one of those times. There was no later.

No one asked about the relationship between her and Lucas during dinner.

It might have had to do with the scorching heat in his eyes every time he looked at her. Or the way he sat two inches from her chair and whispered in her ear every so often. The comments were silly, designed to make her laugh, but every time he leaned in, with his lips close to her ear, laughing didn't happen.

She was consumed with *later* and the lingering taste of him on her lips.

Clearly, she'd underestimated his talent when it came to women. Oh, she wasn't surprised at his ability to kiss a fake fiancée senseless, or how the wickedness of his mouth caused her to forget her own name. No. The surprise lay in how genuine he'd made it feel. Like he'd enjoyed kissing her. Like the audience hadn't mattered.

He'd been doing his job—faking it around other people.

And despite the unqualified awareness that it wasn't real, that it never, ever could be, he'd made her *want* it to be real.

A man who could spin that kind of straw into gold was dangerous.

After dinner, Fran shooed everyone to the huge screened-in porch for coffee. Andy, Matthew and Lucas small talked about work a few feet away, so Cia perched on the wicker love seat overlooking the pool, sipping a cup of coffee to ward off the slight chill darkness had brought. Decaf, because she'd have a hard enough time sleeping tonight as it was. Her body still ached with the unfulfilled promise of Lucas's kiss.

After a conspicuous absence, Fran appeared and joined her.

"This is for you," Fran said, and handed Cia a long, velvet jewelry box. "Open it."

Cia set her coffee aside and sprung the lid, gasping as an eighteen-inch gray pearl and diamond necklace spilled into her hands. "Oh, Fran, I couldn't."

Fran closed Cia's hand over the smooth, cool pearls. "It belonged to my mother and my grandmother before that. My mother's wedding ring went to Ambe—" She cut herself off with a pained glance at Matthew. "My oldest son, but I saved this for Lucas's wife. I want you to have it. It's your something old."

Madre de Dios, how did she refuse?

This was way worse than a villa—it was an heirloom. A beautiful expression of lineage and family and her eyes stung as Fran clasped it around Cia's neck. It hung heavy against her skin, and she couldn't speak.

"It's stunning with your dark hair. Oh, I know it's not the height of fashion," Fran said with a half laugh. "It's old-lady jewelry. So humor me, please, and wear it at the ceremony, then put it away. I'll let Lucas buy you pretty baubles more to your taste."

Cia touched the necklace with the tips of her fingers.

"Thank you." A paltry sentiment compared to the emotion churning through her.

Fran smiled. "You're welcome. At the risk of being tactless, I was crushed you didn't want any family at the wedding. I'm more than happy to pitch in as mother of the bride, if that's part of the issue. You must be missing yours."

Before Cia's face crumpled fully, Lucas materialized at her side and pulled her to her feet. "Mama. I told you Cia doesn't want a big ceremony or any fuss. She doesn't even like jewelry."

Obviously he'd been listening to the conversation. As Fran sputtered, Cia retreated a few mortified steps and tried to be grateful for the intervention.

Her dry eyes burned. No big church wedding for her. No flower girls, chamber music or a delicate sleeveless ecru dress with a princess waist, trimmed in lace. All that signified the real deal, an ability to gift someone with her love and then trust the fates not to rip her happiness away with no warning.

Neither could she in good conscience develop any sort of relationship with Mrs. Wheeler. Better to hurt her now, rather than later.

With her heart in shredded little pieces, Cia unclasped the necklace. "Thank you, but I can't wear this. It doesn't go with a simple civil ceremony. I'm pretty busy at work for the foreseeable future, so lunch is out of the question."

Fran's expression smoothed out as she accepted the return of her box and necklace. "I overstepped. You have my apologies."

"It's fine, Mama. We should go," Lucas said and nodded to the rest of his family, who watched her coolly.

Excellent. Now they all hated her. That's what she should have been going for all night. Then when she and Lucas divorced, he could blame it all on her, and his family would welcome him back into the fold with sympathy and condolences. His mother would say she knew Cia wasn't the right girl for him the moment she'd thrown his great-grandmother's pearls back in her face.

Cia murmured her goodbyes and followed Lucas through the house and out into the starless night.

Once they were settled in their seats, he drove away, as slow as Christmas. But she didn't care so much this time and burrowed into the soft leather, oddly reassured by the scent of pine trees curling around her.

"Thanks, Lucas," she said, and her voice cracked. "For giving me the out with your mother. It was…"

"No problem," he said, jumping in to fill the silence when she couldn't go on. "It takes two to make marriage work, fake or otherwise. I'll do damage control with Mama in the morning. And, darlin', I must confess a real fondness to you calling me Lucas."

His gaze connected with hers, arcing with heat, and the current zinged through the semidark, close quarters of the car. Goose bumps erupted across her skin and her pulse skittered.

All of a sudden, it was later.

Five

Lucas spent the silent, tense ride home revamping his strategy.

Fragileness deepened Cia's shadows, and it was enough to cool his jets. Nothing would have pleased him more than to walk into the house, back her up against the door and start that kiss over again, but this time, his hands would stroke over the hot curves of her body and she'd be naked in short order.

But she wasn't like other women. She wasn't in touch with her sexuality, and he had to live with her—and himself—for the next six months. While he'd like to sink straight into a simple seduction, he had to treat her differently, with no idea what that looked like.

Once they cleared the detached garage, he slid his hand into hers. "Thanks for going to dinner."

Her fingers stiffened. She glanced at him, surprise evident. "You say that like I had a choice."

"You did. With me, you always have a choice. We're partners, not master and slave. So, I'm saying thank you for choosing to spend the evening with my family. It was difficult for you, and I appreciate it."

Her gaze flitted over him, clearly looking for the punch line. "You're welcome, then."

He let go of her hand to open the door. "Now, I don't know about you, but my parents' house always makes me want to let loose a little. I'm half-afraid to move, in case I accidentally knock over one of Mama's precious knickknacks."

Cia smiled, just a little, but it was encouraging all the same. "It is easier to breathe in our house."

Our house. She'd never called it that before, and he liked the sound of it. They were settling in with each other, finding a groove.

He followed her into the living room. "Let's do something fun."

"Like what?"

Instead of answering, he crossed to the entertainment center and punched up the music she'd been playing earlier, when he'd returned home from playing basketball. A mess of electronic noise blasted through the speakers, thumping in his chest. "Dance with me," he yelled over the pulsing music.

"To this?" Disbelief crinkled her forehead. "You haven't even been drinking, white boy."

"Come on." He held out a hand. "You won't dance in public. No one is watching except me, and I can't dance well enough to warrant making fun of you."

He almost fell over when she shrugged and joined him. "I don't like people watching me, but I never said I couldn't dance."

To prove it, she cut her torso in a zigzag and whirled in an intricate move worthy of a music video, hair flying, hands framing her head.

He grinned and crossed his arms, content to be still and watch Cia abandon herself to the beat. His hunch had been right—anyone with her energy would have to be a semicompetent dancer.

After a minute or so of the solo performance, she froze and threw him a look. "You're not dancing."

"Too hard to keep up with that, honey. I'm having a great time. Really. Keep going."

"Not if you're just going to stand there. You asked me to dance *with you*."

Only because he hadn't actually thought she'd say yes. "So I did."

He could be a good sport. But he could not, under any circumstances, dance to anything faster than Brooks & Dunn.

So, he let her make fun of him instead, as he flapped his arms and stomped his feet in what could easily be mistaken for an epileptic seizure. When she laughed so hard she had to hold her sides, nothing but pure Cia floated through her eyes.

The shadows—and the fragileness—had been banished. Score one for Wheeler.

"All right, darlin'. Unless you want to tend to me as I'm laid out flat on my back with a pulled muscle, we gotta dial it down a notch."

She snickered. "What are you, sixty? Shall I run and collect your social security check from the mailbox?"

Before she could protest, he grabbed her hand and twirled her into his arms, body to body. "No, thanks. I've got another idea."

Her arms came up around his waist and she clung to him. Progress. It was sweet.

"Slow dancing?" she asked.

"Slow something, that's for sure." He threaded fingers through her amazing hair and brushed a thumb across her cheek. Her skin was damp from dancing.

As he imagined the glow she'd take on when he got her good and sweaty between the sheets, he went hard. She noticed.

Her eyes widened, and all the color drained from her face as she let go of him faster than a hot frying pan. "It's late. I have a shift in the morning, so I'm about danced out."

All his hard work crumbled to dust under the avalanche of her hang-ups. He let her go with regret. Should have gone with slow dancing, and, as a bonus, she'd still be in his arms. "Sure thing. Big day tomorrow."

The wedding. Realization crept over her expression. "Oh. Yeah. Well, good night."

She fled.

He stalked off to bed and stared at the news for a good couple of hours, unsuccessfully attempting to will away his raging hard-on, before finally drifting off into a restless sleep laced with dreams of Cia wearing his ring and nothing else.

In the morning, he awoke bleary eyed but determined to make some progress in at least one area sorely requiring his attention—work.

The muted hum of the shower in Cia's bathroom traveled through the walls as he passed by.

Cia, wet and naked. Exactly as he'd dreamed.

He skipped breakfast, too frustrated to stay in the house any longer. An early arrival at work wasn't out of line anyway, as Mondays were usually killers. A welcome distraction from the slew of erotic images parading around in his head.

At red lights, he fired off emails to potential clients with the details of new listings. His schedule was insane this week. He had overlapping showings, appraisals and social events he'd attend to drum up new business.

An annoying buzz at the edge of his consciousness kept reminding him of all the balls he had in the air. He'd been juggling the unexpected addition of a full-time personal life and the strain was starting to wear. As long as he didn't drop any balls or clients, everything was cool.

Four o'clock arrived way too fast.

As anticipated, Cia waited for him outside the courthouse,

wearing one of her Sunday-go-to-meeting dresses a grand-mother would envy and low heels.

With her just-right curves and slender legs, put her in a pair of stilettos and a gauzy hot-pink number revealing a nice slice of cleavage…well, there'd be no use for stoplights on the street—traffic would screech to a halt spontaneously. But that wasn't her style. Shame.

Her gaze zeroed in on the bouquet of lilies in his fist. "You just come from a funeral, Wheeler?"

So they were back to *Wheeler* in that high-brow, back-off tone. One tasty kiss-slash-step-forward and forty steps back.

"For you." Lucas offered Cia the flowers. Dang it, he should not have picked them out. If he'd asked Helena to do it, like he should have, when Cia sneered at the blooms, as she surely would, he wouldn't be tempted to throw them down and forget this whole idea. Even a man with infinite patience could only take so much.

But she didn't sneer. Gently, she closed her fingers around the flowers and held them up to inhale the scent.

After a long minute of people rushing by and the two of them standing there frozen, she said, "If you'd asked, I would have said no. But it's kind of nice after all. So you get a pass."

He clutched his chest in a mock heart attack and grinned. "That's why I didn't ask. All brides should have flowers."

"This isn't a real wedding."

She tossed her head and strands of her inky hair fanned out in a shiny mass before falling back to frame her exotic features. This woman he was about to make his wife was such a weird blend of stunning beauty and barbed personality, with hidden recesses of warmth and passion.

What was wrong with him that he was so flippin' attracted to that mix? This marriage would be so much easier if he let it go and worried about stuff he could control, like scaring up new clients.

But he couldn't. He wanted her in his bed, hot and enthusiastic, hang-ups tossed out the window for good.

"Sure it is. We're going to be legally married. Just because it's not traditional doesn't make it less real."

She flipped her free hand. "You know what I mean. A church wedding, with family and friends and cake."

"Is that what you wanted? I would have suffered through a real wedding for you." His skin itched already to think of wearing a tux and memorizing vows. God Almighty...the rehearsal, the interminable ceremony, the toasts. Matthew had undergone it all with a besotted half smile, claiming it was all worth it. Maybe it was if you were in love. "But, darlin', I would have insisted on a real honeymoon."

He waggled his brows, and she laughed nervously, which almost gave him a real heart attack.

A hint of a smile still played around her lips. "A real wedding would have made both of us suffer. That's not what I wanted. I don't have a perfect wedding dress already picked out in hopes my Prince Charming will come along, like other women do. I'm okay with being single for the rest of my life."

"Hold up, honey. You're not a romantic? All my illusions about you have been thoroughly crushed."

Romantic gestures put a happy, glowy expression on a woman's face, and he liked being the one responsible. It was the only sight on this earth anywhere near as pleasurable as watching a woman in the throes of an orgasm he'd given her.

He had his work cut out for him if he wanted to get Cia there.

He put an arm around her waist to guide her inside the courthouse because it was starting to seem as if she wanted to avoid going inside.

The ceremony was quick, and when he slid the slender wedding band of diamonds channel-set in platinum onto her finger, Cia didn't curl her lip. He'd deliberately picked something low-key that she could wear without the glitzy engagement ring. The set had cost more than his car, but he viewed both as an investment. Successful real estate brokers didn't cheap out, and especially now, with Lana's husband on the warpath, every last detail of his life was for show.

With a fast and unsexy kiss, it was over. They were Mr. and Mrs. Wheeler.

The cool, hard metal encircling his finger was impossible to ignore, and he spun it with his pinkie, trying to get used to the weight. Uncomfortable silence fell as they left the courthouse and neither of them broke it. Cia had asked a friend to drop her off, so she rode home with him.

Half-surprised Mama hadn't crashed the event, he called her with the update before he pulled out of the courthouse parking lot. By the time the wheels hit the driveway of the house, Mama had apparently posted the news to Facebook, which then took on a life of its own.

Text messages started rolling in, and he glanced at them as he shifted into Park.

Pete: Dude. Are we still on for bball Sunday? Or do you have to check with the missus?

Justine: REALLY Lucas???? Married???? REALLY????

Melinda: **&^$%. Missed it by that much. Call me the second you get tired of her.

Lucas rolled his eyes. He hadn't spoken to either woman in months. Pete yanked his chain twice a day and had since college.

When Lucas went to shut off his phone, a message came in from Lana: Congrats. Nothing else. The simple half a word spoke volumes and it said, *Poor Lucas, marrying that woman on the rebound.*

"You're popular all of a sudden," Cia said after the fourth beep in a row, and her tone tried and convicted him for a crime he'd not been aware of committing.

"It's just people congratulating us."

And he was done with that. Lana's name popping up on

the screen, after all this time, had unburied disillusionment he'd rather not dwell on.

He hit the phone's off button and dropped it in his pocket, then left the car in the driveway instead of pulling into the garage so it would be easier for Cia to get out.

His efforts to untangle Cia's hang-ups last night had failed. Tonight, he'd try a different approach. "Have dinner with me. To celebrate."

Before he could move, she popped the door and got out. He followed her up the drive and plowed through Amber's fancy flowerbed to beat her to the porch.

"Celebrate what?" she asked, annoyance leaking from her pores. "I was thinking about soaking for an hour or two in a hot bath and going to bed early, actually."

Before she could storm through the entryway, Lucas stopped her with a firm hand on her prickly little shoulder. "Wait."

With an impatient sigh, she turned. "What?"

"Just because you've got your marriage license doesn't mean we're going to walk through this door and never speak again. You realize this, don't you?" He searched her face, determined to find some glimmer of agreement. "This is the beginning, not the end. We've been faking being a happily engaged couple. Now we have to fake being a happily married couple. No, we don't have to put on a performance right now, when no one's around. But to do it in public, trust me, darlin', when I say it will be miles easier if you're not at my throat in private."

Her tight face flashed through a dozen different emotions and finally picked resignation. "Yeah. I know. I owe you an apology. It's been a rough day."

For both of them. "Because you didn't want to get married?"

She shrank a little, as if she couldn't support the heavy weight settling across her shoulders. As if she might shatter into a million shards of razor-sharp glass if he touched her. So he didn't.

But he wanted to, to see if he could soften her up, like during the five seconds he'd had her pliant and breathless in his arms and so off guard she'd actually kissed him back.

"I've been prepared to be married ever since I came up with the idea." Misery pulled at her full mouth. "It's just...I didn't have any idea how hard it would be to get married without my father walking me down the aisle. Me. Who was never going to get married in the first place. Isn't that ridiculous?"

One tear burst loose, trailing down her delicate cheekbone, and he had to do something.

"Hey now," he said, and wrapped his arms around her quivering shoulders, drawing her in close. She let him, which meant she must be really upset. Prickly Cia usually made an appearance when she was uncomfortable about whatever was going on inside her. "That's okay to cry about. Cry all you want. Then I'll get you drunk and take advantage of you, so you forget all about it."

She snorted out a half laugh, and it rumbled pleasantly against his chest. There was something amazing about being able to comfort a woman so insistent on not needing it. He'd grown really fond of soothing away that prickliness.

"I could use a glass of wine," she admitted.

"I have exactly the thing. Come inside." He drew back and smiled when some snap crept back into her watery eyes. "You can drink it while you watch me cook."

"You cook?" That dried up her waterworks in a hurry. "With an oven?"

"Sure enough. I can even turn it on by myself." As he led the way into the kitchen, a squawk cut him off. "Oh, good. Your wedding present is here."

Cia raised her brows at the large cage sitting on the island in the middle of the kitchen. "That's a bird."

"Yep. An African gray parrot." He shed his suit jacket and draped it over a chair in the breakfast nook.

"You're giving me a bird? As a wedding present?"

"Not any bird. African grays live up to fifty years, so you'll have company as you live all by your lonesome the rest of your life. And they talk. I figure anyone who likes to argue as much as you do needed a pet who can argue back. I named her Fergie." He shrugged. "Because you like hip-hop."

Speechless, Cia stared at the man she had married, whom she clearly did not know at all, and tried to make some sort of sound.

"I didn't get you anything," she managed to say.

"That's okay." He unbuttoned his sleeves and rolled them deftly halfway up his tanned forearms, then started pulling covered plates out of the stainless steel refrigerator. "I wasn't expecting anything."

"Neither was I," she mumbled. "Doesn't seem like that matters either way."

She'd never owned a bird and would have to take a crash course on its recommended care. As she peered into the cage, the feathered creature blinked and peered back with intelligent eyes, unafraid and curious. She fell instantly in love.

The psychology of the gift wasn't lost on her. Instead of showering her with expensive, useless presents designed to charm her panties off, he'd opted for a well-thought-out gift. An extremely well-thought-out gift designed for…what?

Every time she thought he was done, Lucas Wheeler peeled back another one of his layers, and every time, it freaked her out a little more.

Regardless, she couldn't lie. "It's the best present I've ever gotten." And she'd remember forever not that her father hadn't been there to give her away, but that her fake husband had given her something genuine on their wedding day. "Thanks, Lucas."

The sentiment stopped him in his tracks, between the

stove and the dishwasher, pan dangling, forgotten, from his hand. That indefinable energy crackled through the air as he treated her to a scorching once-over. "Darlin', you are most welcome."

"Didn't you mention wine?" she asked, to change the subject, and slid onto a barstool edging the granite island.

There was a weird vibe going on tonight, and she couldn't put her finger on it. Alcohol probably wouldn't help.

Lucas retrieved a bottle from the refrigerator. "Sauvignon blanc okay?"

When she nodded, he pulled a corkscrew from a wall hanger, then expertly twisted and wiggled the cork out in one smooth motion. The man did everything with care and attention, and she had a feeling he meant for her to notice. She did. So what?

Yes, his amazing hands would glide over her bare body in a slow seduction and turn her into his sex-starved lover. No question about it.

The real question was why she was envisioning Lucas touching her after simply watching him open wine. Okay. It had nothing to do with wine and everything to do with being in his arms last night. With being kissed and watching him dance like a spastic chicken, draining away all her misery over hurting his mother.

Lucas skirted the barstools and handed her a glass of pale yellow wine. His fingers grazed hers for a shocky second, but it was over so fast, she didn't have time to jerk away. Good thing, or she would have sloshed her drink.

He picked up his own glass and, with his smoky blue-eyed gaze locked with hers, dinged the rims together. "To partnership," he said. "May it be a pleasurable union."

"Successful, you mean. I'll drink to a successful union." As soon as the words came out, she realized her mistake. She and Lucas did not view the world through the same lens.

He took his time swallowing a mouthful of wine, and she

was so busy watching his throat muscles ripple that when his forefinger tipped up her chin, she almost squealed in surprise. His thumb brushed her lips, catching on the lower one, and her breath stuttered when he tilted his head toward hers.

"Darlin'," he said, halting way too close. His whiskey-smooth voice flowed over her. "If you find our union as pleasurable as I intend, I'll consider that a success. Dinner will be ready in forty-five minutes."

A hot flush stole over her cheeks and flooded the places he'd touched. He went back to cooking.

As she watched him chop and sauté and whatever, she had to instruct her stomach to unknot. He'd been messing around, like always. That's all. For Lucas, flirting was a reflex so ingrained he probably didn't realize he was doing it, especially when directing it at his fake wife in whom he had no real interest.

She bristled over his insincerity until Fergie squawked. A fitting distraction from obsessing about the feel of Lucas's thumb on her mouth. She retrieved her laptop from the bedroom and researched what parrots ate while Lucas finished preparing the people food.

"The guy at the pet store said to feed her papaya. They like fruit," Lucas said and refilled her wineglass. "There's one in the refrigerator if you want to cut it up."

She sighed. He'd even bought a papaya. Did the man ever sleep? "Thanks, I will."

Silence fell as she chopped alongside her husband, and it wasn't so bad. She shouldn't be hard on him because he dripped sexiness and made her ache when he looked at her, as if he knew the taste of her and it was delicious. Might as well be ticked over his blue eyes.

The simple celebratory dinner turned into a lavish poolside spread. Lucas led her outside, where a covered flagstone patio edged the elegant infinity pool and palm trees rustled overhead in the slight breeze. Dust coated the closed grill in the top-of-the-line outdoor kitchen, but the landscaping appeared freshly maintained, absent of weeds and overgrown limbs.

Lucas set the iron bistro table with green Fiestaware and served as she took a seat.

"What kind of chicken is this?" she asked and popped a bite into her mouth. A mix of spices and a hint of lime burst onto her tongue.

He shrugged. "I don't know, I made it up. The kitchen is one of the places where I let my creativity roll."

Gee. She just bet she could guess the other place where he rolled out the creativity.

"Oh. I see." She nodded sagely. "Part of your date-night repertoire. Do women take one bite and fall into a swoon?"

"I've never made it for anyone else." His eyes glowed in the dusky light as he stared at her, daring her to draw significance from the statement.

When he stuck a forkful of couscous in his mouth and withdrew it, she pretended like she hadn't been watching his lips.

This was frighteningly close to a conversation over a good bottle of wine, the idea he'd thrown out as the way to get to know each other. But they still weren't dating. Perhaps he should be reminded. "Really? What do you normally make when you have a hot date you want to impress?"

He stopped eating. As he sat back in his chair, he cupped his wineglass and dangled it between two fingers, contemplating her with a reckless smile. "I've never cooked for anyone, either."

She dropped her fork. Now he was being ridiculous. "What, exactly, am I supposed to take from that?"

"Well, you could deduce that I cooked you dinner because I wanted to."

"Why? What's with the parrot and dinner and this—" she waved at the gas torches flaming in a circle around the patio

and pool "—romantic setting? Are you trying to get lucky
or something?"

"Depends." His half-lidded gaze crawled up inside her and
speared her tummy. "How close am I?"

Why couldn't he answer the question instead of talking in
his endless, flirty Lucas-circles?

Oh, no.

His interest in her was real. As real as the hunger in his
expression after kissing her. As real as the evidence of his
arousal while dancing last night. Clues she'd dismissed as…
what? She didn't even know; she'd just ignored them all so
she didn't have to deal with them. Now she did.

Firmly, she said, "We can't have that kind of relationship."
The kind where she gave him a chunk of her heart and he
took it with him when he left. The kind where she'd surrender her hard-won self-reliance, which would happen over her
dead body. "We have an agreement."

"Agreements can be altered." That dangling wineglass between his fingers raked up her nerves and back down again.
He couldn't even be serious about holding stemware.

"This one can't. What if I got pregnant?"

Dios. With fingers trembling so hard she could scarcely
grip the glass, she drained the remainder of her wine and
scouted around for the bottle. There'd be no children in her
future. Life was too uncertain to bring another generation
into it.

"Well, now that's just insulting. What about me suggests
I might be so careless?"

"Arrogance is your preferred method of birth control?"

They were discussing *sex*. She and Lucas were talking
about having sex. Sitting by the pool, eating dinner and talking about sex with her fake-in-name-only-going-away-soon
husband.

"I'm not worried, darlin'. It's never happened before."

She stood so fast the backs of her knees screeched the chair backward until it tipped over. "Well, that's a relief. Please stand back as I become putty in your hands."

He followed her to his feet without fanfare, no more bothered than if they were discussing what color to paint the bathroom.

In one step, he was an inch away, and then he reached out and placed a fingertip on her temple. Lazily, he slid the fingertip down her face, traced the line of her throat and rested it at the base of her collarbone with a tap. "What's going on in there? You're not afraid of getting pregnant."

"Stop touching me." She cocked a brow and refused to move away from the inferno roiling between Lucas's body and hers. He was the one who should back down, not her. Last night, she'd run from this confrontation and look where that had gotten her. "Nothing is going on other than the fact that I'm not attracted to you."

Liar. The hot press of his fingertips against her skin set off an explosion way down low. But wanting someone and being willing to surrender to the feeling were poles apart.

"I don't believe you," he murmured.

He wasn't backing down. His hands eased through her hair, and unmistakable heat edged into his eye.

"What, you think you're going to prove something by kissing me?"

"Yep," he said and dipped his head before she could protest.

For a sixteenth of a second, she considered all possible options, and then his lips covered hers and she went with dissolving into his arms. It was all she could do when Lucas kissed her, his mouth hot and the taste of his tongue sudden and shocking.

His fingers trailed sparklers through her hair and down her spine, molding her against the potent hardness of his body. Clicking them together like nesting spoons, foretelling how sweetly they would fit without clothes.

He angled his head and took her deeper, yanking a long, hard pull from her abdomen. A burst of need uncoiled from a hidden place inside to burn in all the right places. It was real, and it was good. He was good.

So good, she could feel her resistance melting away under the onslaught of his wicked mouth. But she couldn't give in, and, *Dios,* it made her want to weep.

If only he'd kept a couple of those layers hidden. If only she had a way to insulate herself from someone like him. The intensity between them frightened her to the bone, because he had the unique ability to burrow under her defenses and take whatever he wanted.

Then he'd leave her empty, and she'd worked too hard to put herself back together after the last disastrous attempt at a relationship.

She broke away, wrenched out of his arms and rasped, "All that proves is you've practiced getting women naked."

His face was implacable and his shoulders rigid beneath the fabric of his slate-gray button-down. He cleared his throat. "Darlin', why are you fighting this so hard? At first I thought it was because you've been around so much misery, but there's something else going on here."

"Yeah. Something else, like I don't want to. Is your ego so inflated you can't fathom a woman not being interested in you?"

He laughed. "Hon, if that's how you kiss a guy you're not interested in, I'll lick a sardine. Pick a different card."

How dare he throw her own phrase back in her face.

"This is funny to you? How's this for a reason? You might very well be the hottest male on the planet, but I am not willing to be your latest conquest, Wheeler." Her hands clenched into fists and socked against his chest. For emphasis. And maybe to unleash some frustration. He didn't move an iota.

For who knew what ill-advised reason, he reached out, but then he wisely stopped shy of her face. "Is it so difficult to believe you intrigue me and I simply want to unwrap the rest of you?"

"Yeah. It is." She crossed her arms to prevent any more unloading of frustration. His chest was as hard as his head. And other places. "You're feeling deprived. Go find one of the women who text messaged you earlier in the car and scratch your itch with her, because I'm not sleeping with you."

A smile curved his mouth, but the opposite of humor flashed through his steely gaze. "In case it's slipped your mind, I'm married. The only person I'll be sleeping with for the next six months is my wife."

Panic spurted at the back of her throat. Upon meeting her for the first time, he'd kissed her hand—how had she not considered that his old-fashioned streak didn't end there?

Of course, he'd also flat-out told her he wouldn't sleep with another woman while she wore his ring. "Your wife just turned you down flat."

"For tonight anyway."

His supreme confidence pricked at her temper. So he thought he could seduce away her resistance?

"For forever. Honestly, I don't care if you sleep with someone else. It's not really cheating."

The sudden image sprang to mind of Lucas twined with another woman, the way he'd been with her on the bed, his mouth open and heated against the tramp's throat, then kissing her senseless and dipping a clever hand under her clothes.

Her stomach pitched. Ridiculous. She didn't care what he did. She really didn't.

"I care," he said, his silky voice low.

"Why? This isn't a real marriage. You aren't in love with me. You barely like me."

"We're legally married. That makes it really cheating, whether I've had you naked and quivering in my arms or not. Have I made my position clear enough?" Fierceness tightened his mouth and scrunched his eyes and had her faltering.

Anger. It was so foreign, so wrong on Lucas, she didn't know what to do with it.

"I think so." She swallowed against a weird catch in her throat. So, maybe he wasn't quite the horn dog she'd assumed. "Are you clear on my position?"

"Crystal."

Relieved he wasn't going to push some macho, possessive sexual agenda on her, she nodded. "Great. I'm glad we talked this out. It's incredibly important that we handle this fake marriage like rational adults. Now we can go forward as we've discussed, as pure business associates, without any additional complications. Agreed?"

Reflected torchlight danced in his eyes, obscuring his true thoughts. He leaned in and motioned her closer.

With his lips almost touching her earlobe, he said succinctly, "Sweetheart, the only thing I plan to do going forward is regroup. And then, my darlin' Mrs. Wheeler, all bets are off."

He turned on his heel and left her on the patio. She had the distinct impression he was both mad *and* plotting how to get even.

Six

Lucas waited almost a week before cornering the lioness in her den, partially because he'd been hustling his tail off eighteen hours a day to secure at least one elusive client—which had failed miserably—and partially because Cia needed the distance. Pushing her was not the right strategy. She required delicacy and finesse. And patience. God Almighty, did she ever require patience. But when her thorny barriers came tumbling down…well, experience told him she'd be something else once she felt safe enough to let loose. He'd gladly spent a good chunk of unrecoverable work hours dreaming up ways to provide that security.

He did appreciate a challenge. No woman he'd ever romanced had forced him to up his game like she did. He'd have sworn on a stack of Bibles that kind of effort would have him bowing out before sunset. Not this time.

Cia's routine hadn't varied over the past week, so she'd be home from the shelter around four. Usually, he was mired in paperwork in the study or on a conference call or stuffing food in his mouth while doing research as he prepared for a late meeting with a potential client—all activities he could have done at the office.

But he'd developed the habit of listening for her, to be sure she and her zero-to-sixty-in-four-point-two-seconds car made it home in one piece.

Today, he waited in the kitchen and talked to Fergie, who so far only said "hello," "goodbye" and imitated the microwave timer beep so perfectly he almost always turned to open it before realizing she'd duped him. He'd been trying to get her to say "Lucas," but Fergie might be more stubborn than her owner.

When Cia walked in the door, hair caught up in a sassy ponytail, he grinned but kept his hands by his sides instead of nestling her into his arms to explore that exposed neck.

A woman named Dulciana had to have a sweet, gooey center, and he itched to taste it.

"Hey," she said in wary surprise. They hadn't spoken since she'd laid down the law during his aborted celebratory poolside dinner. "What's up?"

"I have a favor to ask," he said. It was better to get to the point since she'd already figured out he wanted something. Being married to Mrs. Psych Minor kept him honest. When the woman at the heart of the challenge was onto him, it made things so much more interesting.

Guarded unease snapped her shoulders back. "Sure. What is it?"

"WFP sold a building to Walrich Enterprises a few months ago, and they're having a ribbon cutting tonight. I'd like to take you."

"Really?" Her forehead bunched in confusion. "Why?"

He swallowed a laugh. "You're my wife. That's who you take to social stuff for work. Plus, people would speculate why I attended solo after just getting married."

"Tell them I had to work." She cocked her head, swinging that ponytail in a wide pendulum, taunting him. So she wanted to play, did she?

"I used that excuse at the last thing I went to. If everyone was curious before, they're rabid now. You don't have much of a social presence as it is, and you're going to get labeled a recluse if you keep hiding out."

"You didn't ask me to go to the last thing." She smiled sweetly enough, but he suspected it was a warning for what would be an excellent comeback. "If I get a reclusive reputation, seems like we might revisit who's to blame."

Yep. She got the first point in this match. But he was getting the next one. "The last thing was boring. I did you a favor by letting you skip it, so you owe me. Come to the ribbon cutting tonight."

"Wow. That was so slick, I didn't see it coming." She crossed her arms, tightening her T-shirt—sunny yellow today—over her chest. "I'd really prefer to skip it, if it's all the same."

With a couple of drunken ballerina sidesteps, she tried to skirt him.

"Cia." He easily stepped in front of her, halting her progress and preventing her from slamming the door on the conversation.

Her irises transformed into deep pools of blue. "You called me 'Cia.' Are you feeling okay?"

His brow quirked involuntarily as he filed away how mesmerizing her eyes became when he called her Cia. It was worth a repeat. "This is important or I wouldn't have asked. You proposed this marriage as a way to rebuild my reputation. That's not going to happen by taking a picture of our marriage license and posting it on the internet. With my nice, stable wife at my side during this event tonight, people will start to forget about Lana."

With a sigh, she closed her lids for a beat. "Why did you have to go and make the one logical point I can't argue with?

Let's pretend I say yes. Are you going to complain about my outfit all night?"

Here came the really tricky part. "Not if you wear the dress I bought you."

Fire swept through her expression, and she snapped, "I specifically asked you not to buy me clothes."

"No, you ordered me not to, and I ignored you. Wear the dress. The guests are the cream of society."

"And you don't want to be ashamed to be seen with me." Hurricane force winds of fury whipped through her frame, leaving him no doubt she'd gladly impale him with a tree limb or two if her path happened to cross them.

"Darlin', come on." He shook his head. "You'd be gorgeous in pink-and-teal sofa fabric, and I'd stand next to you all night with pride. But I want you to be comfortable alongside all those well-dressed people. Appearance is everything to them."

"To them. What about you? Are you that shallow, too?" Her keen gaze flitted over him.

"Appearances aren't everything, but they are important. That's what a reputation is. Other people's view of how you appear to them, which may or may not reflect reality, and that's what makes the world go round. All you can do is present yourself in the best possible light."

Her ire drained away, and a spark of understanding softened her mouth. "That's why you got so angry when I said I didn't care if you slept with other women. Because of how it would look."

And here he thought he'd covered up that unexpected temper flare. Must need more practice. He rarely let much rile him, and it was rarer still to let it show. A temporary, in-name-only wife shouldn't have that kind of effect. He shrugged. "People talk and it hurts, no matter how you slice it. I would never allow that to happen to you because of me."

If Lana had been of the same mind, he'd never have met

this fierce little conquistador now called Mrs. Lucas Wheeler. A blessing or a curse?

"I'm sorry I suggested it. It was insensitive." With a measured exhale, she met his gaze. "I'll go. But I want to see the dress before I agree to wear it. It's probably too big."

Well, then. She'd conceded not just the point but the whole match. A strange tightness in his chest loosened. "It's hanging in your closet. Try it on. Wear it if you like it. Throw it in the trash if you hate it. We should leave around seven, and I'll take you to dinner afterward." He risked squeezing her hand, and the cool band of her wedding ring impressed his palm. "Thanks. I promise you'll have fun tonight."

She rolled her eyes. "I don't even want to know how you plan to guarantee that." She let their hands slip apart and successfully navigated around him to leave the kitchen. Over her shoulder, she shot the parting volley. "See you at seven-ten."

Later that night, Lucas hit the ground floor of their house at six fifty-five. When Cia descended the stairs at seven on the dot, his pulse stumbled. Actually *stumbled*. He'd known the floor-length red sheath would look amazing on her as soon as he'd seen it in the window.

Amazing didn't cover it. She'd swept her hair up in a sexy mess of pins and dark locks and slipped black stockings over legs that peeped through the skirt's modest slit.

"Darlin', you take my breath away," he called up with a grin contrived to hide the fact that he was dead serious. His lungs hurt. Or at least something in his chest did.

Compared to his vivacious wife, Lana was a pale, lackluster phantom flitting along the edges of his memory.

"Yeah, well, I have a feeling when I trip over this long dress, I'll take *my* breath away, too," she said as she reached the ground floor. "Did you seriously tell me to throw Versace in the trash?"

The distinctive scent of coconut and lime wafted over him.

"Not seriously." His mouth was dry. He needed a drink. Lots of drinks. "I knew you wouldn't hate it."

"Don't pat yourself on the back too hard. I'm only wearing it because the price tag is equal to the GDP of some small countries. It would be wrong to throw it away." Sincerity oozed from her mouth. But he was onto her.

He stared her down. Even in heels, she only came up to his nose. "I still have the receipt. Pretty sure the store would take it back. Run upstairs and change. I'll wait."

"All right, all right." She spit out a bunch of Spanish, and danged if it wasn't sexy to watch her mouth form the foreign words. Then she sighed, and it was long-suffering. "It's beautiful and fits like a dream. Because your ego isn't big enough already, I will also admit you have an excellent eye for style. If you undress a girl as well as you dress one, your popularity with the ladies is well deserved."

A purifying laugh burst out of him. He'd missed sparring with her this past week and the mental gymnastics required. When she engaged him brain to brain, it thoroughly turned him on.

Something was definitely wrong with him.

"Well, now. As it happens, I believe I'm pretty proficient at both. Anytime you care to form your own opinion, let me know. Ready?"

She laughed and nodded. Obviously, something was wrong with both of them, because he'd bet every last dollar that she enjoyed their heated exchanges as much as he did, though she'd likely bite off her tongue before saying so. Which would be a shame since he had a very specific use in mind for that razor-sharp tongue of his wife's.

The ribbon-cutting ceremony at Walrich's new facility was packed. People talked to Lucas, and he talked back, but he couldn't for the life of him recall the conversations because he spent the evening entranced by his wife's bare neck.

Since they were in public, he had every reason to touch

her whenever the inclination hit, which happened often. The torch-red dress encased her slim body with elegance, and the sight of her very nice curves knifed him in the groin.

Sure he'd bought women clothes before, but not for a woman who lived under his roof and shared his last name. Everything felt bigger and more significant with Cia, even buying her an age-appropriate dress. Even bringing her to a social event with the strict intent of jump-starting his reputation rebuild.

Even casually resting his hand on the back of her neck as they navigated the room. The silk of her skin against his fingers bled through him with startling warmth. Startling because the response wasn't only sexual.

And that just wasn't possible.

"Let's go," he told Cia. Matthew could work potential clients, which was his strength anyway. "We've done enough mingling."

"Already?" She did a double take at the expression on his face. "Okay. Where are we going for dinner?"

He swore. Dinner put a huge crimp in his intent to distance himself immediately from the smell of coconut and lime.

But if he bailed, whatever had just happened when he touched Cia would stick in his mind, nagging at him. Not cool. That fruity blend was messing with his head something fierce.

What was he thinking? He couldn't leave the schmoozing to Matthew like he used to. Cia hadn't balked at attending the ribbon cutting. What kind of coward let his wife do all the hard work?

The best way to handle this divorce deal, and his disturbing attraction to the woman on his arm, was obviously to remember the Lucas Wheeler Philosophy of Relationships—have a lot of sex and have a lot of fun, preferably at the same time.

This was a temporary liaison with a guaranteed outcome, and besides, he was with an inarguably beautiful woman. What other kind of response was there except sexual?

Shake it off, Wheeler.

"A place with food," he finally said.

Cia eyed her decadently beautiful husband, who should be required by law to wear black tie every waking hour, and waited a beat for the rest of the joke. It never came.

She hadn't seen Lucas in a week and had started to wonder exactly how mad she'd made him by the pool. Then he'd appeared and asked her pretty please to attend this boring adult prom, which she couldn't legitimately refuse, so she hadn't. For her trouble, he'd spent the evening on edge and not himself. "Great. Places with food are my favorite."

Matthew Wheeler materialized in front of them before they could head for the exit.

Lucas glanced at his brother. "What's the climate with Moore?"

Since Matthew was pretending she was invisible, Cia openly studied her authoritative, remote brother-in-law. A widower, Lucas had said, and often dateless, as he was tonight. Clearly by choice, since any breathing woman would find Matthew attractive—as long as he didn't stand next to Lucas. When he did, he was invisible, too.

"Better than I expected." Matthew signaled a waiter and deposited his empty champagne flute on the tray. "He's on the hook. I booked reservations in your name at the Mansion for four. Take Moore and his wife to dinner on me. Since closing the deal is your forte, I'll bow out. Bring it home."

As if they'd practiced it a dozen times, Lucas kissed Cia's temple, and she managed to lean into it like his lips weren't hotter than a cattle brand. Nothing like a spark of Lucas to liven up the prom.

Not that she'd know anything about prom. She'd missed that and the last half of senior year, thanks to the accident that had taken her parents.

"Do me a favor," Lucas said, "and hang out with Matthew

for a minute. Looks like we might have different plans for the evening."

Then he strode off through the crowd to go work his magic on some unsuspecting guy named Moore.

Matthew watched her coolly through eyes a remarkably close shade to Lucas's. "Having a good time, Cia?"

Oh, so she'd miraculously reappeared. But she didn't mistake the question as friendly. "Yes, thank you. Your clients are impressive."

"What few we have, I suppose." His shrewd gaze narrowed. "I'll be honest. I have no idea what got into Lucas by marrying you, but I see the way he looks at you and I hope there's at least a chance you're making him happy."

What way did Lucas look at her—like a spider contemplating a particularly delectable fly? His brother should find a pair of glasses. She narrowed her gaze right back. "So, you'll hunt me down if I hurt him?"

He laughed, and the derisive note reminded her again of Lucas. They didn't look so much alike but they did have a similar warped sense of humor, apparently.

"I highly doubt you have the capacity to hurt Lucas. He's pretty good at staying emotionally removed from women. For example, he didn't blink when he found out about Lana. Just moved right along to the next one."

As warnings went, it was effective—if she'd been harboring some romantic illusion about Lucas's feelings toward her. "How many of the next ones did Lucas marry?"

"Touché." Her brother-in-law eyed her and then nodded to an older couple who'd swept past them on the way to the bar. "I know you're not after Lucas's money. I checked out you and your trust fund. I'm curious, though, why didn't you stay at Manzanares?"

The loaded question—and Matthew's bold and unapologetic prying—stomped on her defenses. "I worked there for a year to appease my grandfather. I'm probably the only one he'd trust to take over." Shrugging, she wrapped it up. She didn't owe him any explanations. "It's not my passion, so he plans to live forever, I guess."

Matthew didn't smile. Thank goodness Lucas had been the one in need of a wife and not his brother. There was a brittleness to Matthew Wheeler, born of losing someone who meant everything, and she recognized it all too well.

In contrast, Lucas played at life, turning the mundane fun, and he smiled constantly in a sexy, self-assured way, which sometimes caught her with a lovely twist in the abdomen. That was the thing she liked most about him.

Dios. When had that happened?

"Family may not mean much to you, Cia. But it's everything to us." Matthew's expression hardened, and she revised her opinion. The frozen cerulean of his irises scarcely resembled the stunning smoky blue of Lucas's. "Lana punched a hole in Lucas's pride, which is easily dismissed, but in the process, she nearly destroyed a century of my family's hard work. That's not so easily overcome. Be an asset to him. That's all I'll say."

Matthew clammed up as Lucas rejoined them with a deceptively casual hand to the place where her neck and shoulder met. The dress she wore nearly covered her from head to foot and yet her husband managed to find the one bare spot on her body to brush with his electric fingertips.

She'd missed him. And no way would she ever admit it.

"Dinner's on," he told Matthew. "I'll call you later."

Matthew's advice echoed in her head as she let Lucas lead her to his car. Well, she was here, wasn't she? There was also a contract somewhere in Lucas's possession granting him the sales rights to the Manzanares complex, which Abuelo had gladly signed.

Her relationship with Lucas was as equitable as possible. How much more of an asset could she be?

Regardless, all through dinner she thought about Fergie.

And the house. She wore the Versace and the diamond rings her husband had selected. The scales in her mind unbalanced, and she was ashamed Matthew had to be the one to point out how little she'd given Lucas in return for throwing his strengths on the table.

She'd been so focused on making sure she didn't fall for his seduce-and-conquer routine, she'd forgotten they had an agreement.

Their partnership wasn't equitable at all, not with her shrewish behavior and giving him a hard time about attending a social event. She should have been glad to attend, but she wasn't because her husband was too much of a temptation to be around.

Lucas didn't try to kiss her or anything at the end of the evening, and she reminded herself four times how pleased she was the back-off messages were sinking in.

She slept fitfully that night and woke in the morning to dreary storm clouds, which she should have taken as a warning to stay in bed.

A young Hispanic woman in a crisp uniform was scrubbing the sink when Cia walked into the kitchen.

The girl smiled. *"Buenos días, señora."*

Cia looked over her shoulder automatically and then cursed. *She* was the *señora,* at least for the next few months. "Good morning," she responded in Spanish. "I'm sorry, I didn't realize Mr. Wheeler hired a maid."

Of course if he'd bothered to tell her, she would have. Men.

"I'm to come three days a week, with strict instructions you must be happy with my work." The girl bobbed her head and peeled yellow latex gloves from her hands, which she dropped into the sink. "I've already cleaned the master suite. With your permission, I'd like to show you what I've done."

"Sure." Cia was halfway to the stairs before the raucous clang of a big, fat warning bell went off in her head. "You, um, cleaned the master suite? The bathroom, too?" Where there was a noticeable lack of cosmetics, hair dryer or conditioner.

Her heart flipped into overtime.

Satanás en un palo. The maid had cleaned Lucas's bedroom while Cia slept in her room down the hall. They might as well have put out a full-page ad in the *Dallas Morning News*—Mr. and Mrs. Lucas Wheeler Don't Share a Bedroom.

While the maid politely pointed out the sparkling tile and polished granite vanity in the master bathroom, Cia listened with about a quarter of her attention and spent the other three-quarters focusing on how to fix it.

Lucas had royally screwed up. Not on purpose. But still.

"So you'll be back on Wednesday?" Cia asked when the maid finished spouting about the cleaning process.

"Tomorrow, if acceptable. This week, I have Wednesday off. And then back again on Friday."

Of course she'd be back tomorrow. "Fine. That's fine. Your work is exceptional, and I'm very pleased with it. Please let me know when you've finished for the day."

The maid nodded and went off to clean, oblivious to Cia's ruined day. Cia called the shelter to let them know she'd be unavoidably late and sent Lucas a text message: Come home before eight. I have to talk to you.

The second the maid's compact car backed out of the driveway, Cia started transferring her clothes into Lucas's bedroom. Fortunately, there was a separate, empty walk-in closet inside the bathroom. It took twelve trips, fourteen deep breaths and eight minutes against the wall in a fetal position, forehead clamped between her fingers, to get all her clothes moved.

Toiletries she moved quickly with a clamped jaw, and then had to stop as soon as she opened the first dresser drawer, which contained tank tops and drawstring shorts. Sleepwear.

She'd have to sleep in the same room with Lucas. On the floor. Because there was no way she'd sleep in the same bed.

No way she'd sleep in it even if he wasn't in it. No doubt the sheets smelled all pine-tree-like and outdoorsy and Lucas-y.

And, boy, wouldn't the floor be comfortable? Especially with Lucas breathing and rustling and throwing the covers off his hard, tanned body as he slept a few feet away.

God, he better be several feet away. What if he pounced on the opportunity to try to sweet-talk her into bed?

What if? Like there was a snowball's chance he'd pass up the opportunity. And after last night, with the dress and the warm hand on her shoulder all evening and the way he kept knocking down her preconceptions of him, there was a tiny little corner of her mind afraid she'd let herself be swept away by the man she'd married.

Her feminine parts had been ignored for far too long—but not long enough to forget how much of a mess she'd been after the last time she'd jumped into bed, sure that *this* was finally the right man to heal the pain from losing her parents, only to scare yet another one away with colossal emotional neediness.

She was pretty passionate about whatever she touched, and there weren't many men who could handle it, especially not when it was coupled with an inadvertent drive to compensate for the gaping wound in her soul. Until she figured out how to be in a relationship without exposing all the easy-to-lose parts of herself, the best policy was never to get involved—or to get out as quickly as possible.

There had to be another way to solve this problem with the maid besides sleeping in the same room with Lucas. What if she moved her stuff to Lucas's room and got ready for bed there but slept in her room? She could get up early the days the maid came and make up the bed like she'd never been there. Or maybe she could pretend the maid hadn't met her standards and dismiss her. Maybe moving her stuff was a total overreaction.

Her phone beeped. She pulled it from her back pocket. Incoming text from Lucas: What's wrong? What do you need to talk about?

She texted him back: It's an in-person conversation. BTW, how did you find the maid?

In thirty seconds, the message alert beeped again. Lucas: She just started working for my mother and came highly recommended by your grandfather. Why?

Abuelo. She moaned and sank to the floor, resting her forehead on the open drawer full of sleepwear.

Well, if anything, she'd underreacted. The maid was her grandfather's spy, commissioned to spill her guts about Cia's activities at the shelter, no doubt. Abuelo probably didn't even anticipate the coup of information coming his way about the living arrangements.

It was too late to dismiss her. Imagine the conversation where she said a maid who was good enough for Lucas's mother wasn't good enough for Cia. And was she really going to fire a maid who probably sent at least fifty percent of her take-home pay back to extended family in Mexico?

Not only did she and Lucas need to be roommates by tomorrow, she'd have to come up with a plausible reason why they hadn't been thus far and a way to tell the maid casually.

With a grimace, she weaved to her feet and started yanking tank tops out of the drawer, studiously avoiding thoughts about bedrooms, Lucas, beds and later.

Beep. Lucas: Still there? What's up?

Quickly, she tapped out a response: Yeah. No prob with the maid. Late for work. Talk 2U tonight. Have a good day.

She cringed. Wait until he found out his wife telling him to have a good day was the least of the surprises in store.

Seven

Lucas rescheduled three showings he could not afford to put off and pulled into the garage at home by five, thanks to no small effort and a white-knuckle drive at ten over the speed limit. Suspense gnawed at his gut. Something was wrong, and Cia being so closemouthed about it made it ten times worse. Most women considered it worthy of a hysterical phone call if the toilet overflowed or if they backed the car into the fence. With his wife, the problem could range from serious, like the shelter closing down, to dire, like her grandfather dying.

Cia's car wasn't in the garage or the driveway, so he waited in the kitchen. And waited. After forty-five minutes, it was clear she must be working late. More than a little irritated, he went upstairs to change. As he yanked a T-shirt over his head, he caught sight of the vanity through the open bathroom door.

The counter had been empty when he left this morning. Now it wasn't.

A mirrored tray sat between the twin sinks, loaded with

lotion and other feminine stuff. He picked up the lotion and opened it to inhale the contents. Yep. Coconut and lime.

In four seconds, he put the cryptic text messages from Cia together with the addition of this tray, a pink razor, shaving cream and at least six bottles of who knew what lining the stone shelf in the shower.

The maid had spooked Cia into moving into the master bedroom. Rightly so, if the maid had come recommended by Cia's grandfather, a detail he hadn't even considered a problem at the time.

Man, he should have thought of that angle long ago. In a few hours, Cia might very well be sleeping in his bed.

He whistled a nameless tune as he meandered back to the kitchen. No wonder Cia was avoiding home as long as possible, because she guessed—correctly—he'd be all over this new development like white on rice. Her resistance to the true benefit of marriage was weakening. Slowly. Tonight might be the push over the edge she needed.

At seven o'clock, he sent her a text message to find out what time she'd be home. And got no answer.

At eight o'clock he called, but she didn't pick up. In one of her texts, she'd mentioned being late for work. Maybe she'd stayed late to make up for it. He ate a roast beef sandwich and drank a dark beer. Every few bites, he coaxed Fergie to say his name.

But every time he said, "Lucas. Looo-kaaaas," she squawked and ruffled her feathers. Sometimes she imitated Cia's ringtone. But mostly the parrot waited for him to shove a piece of fruit through the bars, then took it immediately in her sharp claws.

At nine-thirty, Lucas realized he didn't know the names of Cia's friends and, therefore, couldn't start calling to see if they'd heard from her. There was avoidance, and then there was late.

Besides, Cia met everything head-on, especially him. Radio silence wasn't like her.

At eleven o'clock, as he stared at the TV while contemplating a call to the police to ask about accidents involving a red Porsche, the automatic garage door opener whirred.

A beat later, Cia trudged into the kitchen, shoulders hunched and messy hair falling in her face.

"Hey," he said.

"Hey," she repeated, her voice thinner than tissue paper. "Sorry. I got your messages."

"I was kind of worried."

"I know." The shadows were back in full force, and there was a deep furrow between her eyes he immediately wanted to soothe away.

"I'm sorry," she repeated. "It was unavoidable. I'm sure you saw my stuff in your room."

None of this seemed like the right lead-up to a night of blistering passion. "I did. So we're sharing a bedroom now?"

She squeezed her temples between a thumb and her middle finger, so hard the nail beds turned white. "Only because it's necessary. Give me fifteen minutes, and then you can come in."

Necessary. Like it was some big imposition to sleep in his bed. He knew a woman or two who'd be there in a heartbeat to take her place. Why couldn't he be interested in one of them instead of his no-show wife, who did everything in her power to avoid the best benefit of marriage?

Fearful of what he might say if he tried to argue, he let her go without another word and gave her twenty minutes, exactly long enough for his temper to flare.

He was married, mad and celibate, and the woman responsible for all three lay in his bed.

When he strode into the bedroom, it was dark, so he felt his way into the bathroom, got ready for bed and opted to sleep naked, like normal. This was his room and since she'd moved into it without asking, she could deal with all that entailed.

He hit the button on the TV remote. She better be a heavy sleeper, because he always watched TV in bed, and he wasn't changing his habits to suit anyone, least of all a prickly wife who couldn't follow her own mandate to be home by eight.

The soft light of the flat screen mounted on the wall spilled over the empty bed. He glanced over at it. Yep, empty. Where was she?

A pile of sheets on the floor by the bay windows answered that question. "Cia, what are you doing over there?"

"Sleeping," came the muffled reply from the mass of dark hair half-buried under the pile.

Since she still faced the wall, he turned the volume down on the TV. "You can't sleep on the floor."

"Yes, I can."

"This bed is a California king. Two people could easily sleep in it without touching the entire night." Could. But that didn't necessarily mean he'd guarantee it. Although, given his mood, he was pretty sure he'd have no problem ignoring the unwilling woman in his bed.

After a lengthy pause, she mumbled, "It's your bed. I'm imposing on you. The floor is fine."

The martyr card. Great. A strangled sigh pushed out through his clamped teeth. "Get in the bed. I'll sleep on the floor."

"No. That's not fair. Besides, I like the floor. This carpet is very soft."

"Well, then." Two could play that game. "Since it's so comfortable, I'll sleep on the floor, too."

With a hard yank, he pulled the top sheet out from under the comforter, wrapped it around his waist and threw a pillow on the floor a foot from hers. As he reclined on the scratchy carpet, she rolled over and glared at him.

"Stop being so stubborn, Wheeler. The bed is yours. Sleep in it."

Coconut and lime hit his nose, and the resulting pang to the abdomen put a spike in his temper. "Darlin', you go right ahead and blow every gasket in that pretty little head of yours. I'm not sleeping in the bed when you're on the floor. It's not right."

She made a frustrated noise in her throat. "Why do you always have to be such a gentleman about *everything?*"

"'Cause I like to irritate you," he said easily.

She flipped back to face the wall. As he was about to snap out more witticisms, her shoulders started shaking.

"Hey," he called. "Are you crying?"

"No," she hissed, followed by a wrenching sob.

"Aw, honey, please don't cry. If it'll make you feel better, you can call my mother and yell at her for teaching me manners. Either way, I'm not sleeping in the bed unless you do."

This pronouncement was greeted with a flurry of sobbing. Every ounce of temper drained away.

Obviously, his manners weren't as well practiced as he'd bragged, and he'd been too worked up to remember arguing and prickliness were Cia's way of deflecting the comfort she sorely needed but refused to ask for.

He scuttled forward and cursed the binding sheet and sandpaper carpet impeding his progress, but finally he wormed close enough to gather her in his arms. "Shh. It's okay."

She stiffened as the war going on inside her spread out to encompass her whole body. Then, all at once, she surrendered, melting into a puddle of soft, sexy woman against him, nestling her head on his shoulder and settling her very nice backside tight against his instantly firm front side.

Hell on a horse. He'd only been trying to get her to stop crying. He honestly expected her to kick him away. The sheet chafed against his bare erection, spearing his lower half with white-hot splinters. He sucked in a breath and let it out slowly. It didn't help.

Prickly Cia he could resist all day long. Vulnerable Cia got under his skin.

Her trim body was racked with sobs against his, yet he was busy trying to figure out what she had on under that pile of sheets. *Moron.*

He shut his eyes and pulled her tighter into his arms, where she could sob to her heart's content for as long as it took. His arousal ached every time he moved, but he stroked her hair and kept stroking until she fell still a million excruciating years later.

"Sorry." She sniffed into the sudden silence. "I'm just so tired."

He kept stroking her hair in case the torrent wasn't over. And because he liked the feel of its dark glossiness. "That wasn't tired. That was distraught."

"Yeah." A long sigh pushed her chest against his forearm. "But I'm tired, too. So tired I can't pretend I hate it when you calm me down. I don't know what's worse, the day I had or having to admit you've got the touch."

His hand froze, dark strands of her hair still threaded through his fingers. "What's so bad about letting me make you feel better?"

She twisted out of his arms and impaled him with the evil eye. "I hate being weak. I hate you seeing my weaknesses. I hate—"

"Not being able to do everything all by yourself," he finished and propped his head up with a hand since she was no longer curled in his arms. "You hate not being a superhero. I get it. Lie down now and take a deep breath. Tell me what tall building you weren't able to leap today, the one that made you cry."

Her constant inner battle played out over her face. She fought everything, even herself. No wonder she was tired.

With a shuddery sigh, she lay on the pillow, facing him, and light from the TV highlighted her delicate cheekbones. Such a paradox, the delicacy outside veiling the core of steel inside. Something hitched in his chest.

Oh, yeah. This strong woman hated falling. But he liked being the only one she would let catch her.

"One of the women at the shelter..." she began and then faltered. Threading their fingers together, he silently encouraged her to go on. A couple of breaths later, she did. "Pamela. She went back to her husband. That bastard broke her arm when he shoved her against a wall. And she went back to him. I tried to talk her out of it. For hours. Courtney talked to her, too. Nothing we said mattered."

He vaguely recalled Courtney was Cia's friend and also her partner in the new shelter. A psychologist. "You can't save everyone."

She pulled their fingers apart. "I'm not trying to save everyone. Just Pamela. I work with these women every day, instilling confidence. Helping them see they can be self-sufficient..." Her voice cracked.

She looked at this as failure—as her failure. Because these women, and what she hoped to accomplish with them, meant something, and she believed in both. It went way past fulfilling her mother's wishes. Her commitment was awe inspiring.

The line between her eyes reappeared. "She threw it all out to go back to a man who abused her. He might kill her next time. What could possibly be worth that?"

"Hope," he said, knowing his little psych minor couldn't see past her hang-ups. "Hope people can change. Hope it might be different this time."

"But why? She has to know it's got a one hundred percent certainty of ending badly."

"Honey, I hate to rain on your parade, but people naturally seek companionship. We aren't meant to be alone, despite all your insistence to the contrary. This Pamela needs to hope the person she chose to marry is redeemable so they can get on with their lives together. Without hope, she has nothing."

Hair spilled into her face when she shook her head. "That's not true. She has herself, the only person she can truly rely on. The only person who can make sure she's taken care of."

"Are you talking about Pamela or Cia?"

"Don't go thinking you're smart for shoving a mirror in my face. It's true for both of us, and I've never had any illusions about my beliefs, particularly in relation to men."

"Illusions, no. Blind spots, yes." He ventured a little closer. "You're so black-and-white. You saw the trust clause and assumed your grandfather intended to manipulate you into a marriage where you'd be dominated by a man. You said it yourself. He wants you to be taken care of. Allowing someone to take care of you isn't weakness."

Her mouth tightened. "I can take care of myself. I have money, I have the ability to—"

"Darlin', there's more to being cared for than money." He swept a lock of hair off her shoulder and used the proximity as an excuse to run his hand across her silky skin again. "You have physical needs, too."

"Oh, my God. You do indeed have a gift. How in the world did you manage to drop sex into this conversation?"

He grinned in spite of the somber tone of their illuminating conversation. "Hey, I didn't say anything about sex. That was you. I was talking about holding you while you cry. But if you want to talk about sex, I could find some room in my schedule. Maybe start with telling me the most sensitive place on your body. Keep in mind, I'll want to test it, so be honest."

She smacked him on the arm without any real heat. "You're unbelievable. I'm not having sex with you simply because we've been forced into sharing a room."

Touching him on purpose. Would wonders never cease? He caught her gaze. "Then do it because you want to."

Her frame bristled from crown to toe, and the sheet slipped

down a few tantalizing inches. "I don't want to, Wheeler! You think you're God's gift to women and it never occurs to you some of us are immune to all your charm and…and—" her hungry gaze skittered over his chest, which he had not hidden under a sheet mummy-style, like she had "—sexiness. Stop trying to add another notch to your bedpost."

Could she have protested any more passionately? "Okay."

"Okay?" One eye narrowed and skewered him. "Just like that, you're giving up?"

"That was not an okay of concession. It was an okay, it's time to change the subject. Roll over."

"What? Why?"

A growl rumbled through his chest. "Because I said so. You need to relax or you'll never go to sleep. If you don't go to sleep, you'll keep arguing with me, and then I won't sleep. I'm just going to massage your shoulders. So shut up and do it."

Warily, she rolled, and he peeled the sheet from her as she spun, resetting it at her waist. Tank top with spaghetti straps. Not the sexiest of nightclothes, but when he lifted the dark curtain of hair away from her neck, the wide swath of bare skin from the middle of her back up to her hairline pleaded for his touch.

So he indulged.

First, he traced the ridges of her spine with his fingertips, imprinting the textures against his skin. Once he reached her neck, he went for her collarbone, following it around to the front and back again.

She felt amazing.

He wanted more of her naked flesh under his fingers. Under his body. Shifting against his skin, surrounding him with a hot paradox of hard and soft.

The stupid floor blocked his reach, so he settled for running his fingers over her exposed arm, trying to gauge whether she'd notice if he slipped the tank top strap off her shoulder.

"What, exactly, are you doing?" She half rolled to face him. "This is the least relaxing massage I've ever had."

"Really?" he asked nonchalantly and guided her back into place. No way was he missing a second of unchecked access to Cia. "Someone who's immune to my charms should have no problem relaxing while I'm impersonally rubbing her shoulders."

"Hmpf." She flipped back to face the wall. Must not hate it too much.

He let the grin spread wide and kneaded her neck muscles. "Darlin', there's no sin in enjoying it when someone touches you."

She snorted but choked on it as his hand slid up the inside of her arm again and a stray finger stroked her breast. He needed the tank top gone and that breast cupped in his palm.

"There is the way you do it," she rasped.

"You know," he said, closing the gap between them, spooning her heated back to murmur in her ear, a millimeter from taking the smooth lobe into his mouth. "I don't for a moment believe I'm God's gift to women. Women are God's gift to man. The female form is the most wonderful sight on earth. The beautiful design of your throat, for example."

He dragged his mouth away from her ear and ran his lips down the column of her neck. "I could live here for a decade and never completely discover all the things I love about it," he said, mouthing the words against her skin.

He was so hard and so ready to sink into her, his teeth hurt.

Her head fell back onto his shoulder, her eyes closed and her lashes fluttered, fully exposing the area under discussion. Her sweet little body arched in wanton invitation, spreading against his. He wanted to dive in, find Dulciana's gorgeous, gooey center and feast on it.

This visceral attraction would be satisfied, here and now.

"Lucas," she breathed, and his erection pulsed. "Lucas, we can't. You have to stop."

"Why?" He slid a hand under her tank top, fanning his palm out on her flat stomach and working it north. Slowly. Familiarizing his fingertips with velvety skin. "And if you use that smart mouth to lie to me again about your lack of interest, I will find something better to do with it."

"I doubt even I could pull off that lie anymore," she said wryly.

The admission was so sweet, he couldn't help it.

He found her lips and consumed them, kissing her with every bit of frustrated, pent-up longing. And God Almighty, her lips parted just enough, and he pushed his tongue into her mouth, tasting her, reveling in the hot slide of flesh.

For a few magnificent seconds she tasted him back, triggering a hard coil of lust.

But then she ripped her lips away, mumbling, "No more," as his thumb brushed the underside of her breast.

She bowed up with a gasp, and his erection tingled. She was so responsive, like it had been ages since she'd... He pulled his hand free and gripped her chin to peer into her eyes. "Hold up a sec. You're not a virgin, are you?"

That would explain a few things.

He let his fingers fall away as she sat up. "My past experience is not the issue. We agreed to keep this business only."

No. No more of this endless circling. *Business only* disappeared eons ago, and she knew it as well as he did.

"Why are you here, in my bedroom? You could have easily moved your stuff and still slept in your room. But you didn't. Your signals are so mixed up, you've even confused yourself. Talk to me, honey. No more pretending. Why the roadblocks, when it's obvious we both want this?"

She crossed her arms and clamped her mouth shut. But then she said, "I don't like being some big challenge. If I give in, you win. Then off you go to your cave to beat your chest and crow over your prize."

"Give in?" He shook his head to clear it. They should both

be naked and using their mouths on each other. Not talking. "You better believe you challenge me. Something fierce, too, I'll admit. You challenge me to be better than I ever thought I could be, to rise to the occasion and go deep so I can keep up. I dig that seven ways to Sunday. Feel what you do to me, Cia."

Her eyes went liquid as he flattened her hand over his thundering heart, and when the muscle under her cool palm flexed, she curled her fingers as if trying to capture his response. She weaved closer, drawn by invisible threads into his space.

"You're so incredibly intelligent," he continued, fighting to keep from dragging her against him and sinking in like he ached to do. She had to choose this on her own. "How have you not figured out that gives you all the power? I'm just a poor, pathetic man who wants to worship at the altar of the goddess."

She hesitated, indecision and longing stamped all over her face. Whatever stopped her from jumping in—and it wasn't dislike of being a challenge—drove the battle inside of her to a fever pitch. She spent way too much energy thinking instead of feeling and way too much time buried in shadows.

And here he was trying to help her fix that, if she'd lay down that stubborn for a minute.

"You're the strongest woman I've ever met, and I like that about you," he said. "We both know strings aren't part of the deal. This is about one thing only. Sex. Fantastic, feel-good, uncomplicated sex. Nobody gets hurt. Everyone has fun. Sounds perfect for an independent woman with a divorce on the horizon, doesn't it?"

"Seducing me with logic. Devious."

"But effective."

The curve of her lips set off a tremor in his gut. "It's getting there."

Hallelujah. He threw his last-ditch inside straight on the table. "Then listen close. Let me take care of you. Physically. You give to your women till it hurts. Take for once. Let me make you feel good. Let me help you forget the rest of the world for a while. Use me, I insist. Do I benefit from it, too? Absolutely. That's what makes for a great partnership."

He'd laid the foundation for a new, mutually beneficial agreement. The next move had to be hers. She needed to be in control of her fate, and he needed to know she could never accuse him of talking her into it.

"Now, darlin', the floor sucks. I'm going to get in that nice, comfortable bed over there and if you want to spend the next few hours being thoroughly pleasured, join me. If not, don't. You make the choice."

Eight

Choice.

Instead of seducing her, Lucas had given her a choice. And with that single empowering act, Cia's uncertainty disappeared.

They were partners—equals—and he'd done nothing but respect that, and respect her, from the very beginning. He got her in ways she'd only begun to realize. Domination was not part of his makeup, and all he wanted from her was to join him in taking pleasure from sex, the way he took pleasure from every aspect of life.

She longed to indulge in the foreign concept, to seize what she wanted—Lucas.

To let his talents wash away all the doubt and frustration and disappointment about Pamela and help Cia forget everything except how he made her feel. He'd stripped the complexity from the equation and, suddenly, sex didn't mean she'd lose something.

The only way Lucas Wheeler could take a chunk of her

soul when he left was if she gave it to him. She wouldn't. Simple as making a choice. Who knew the secret to avoiding emotional evisceration was to lay out divorce terms first?

She stood and crossed the carpet with sure steps until her knees hit the side of the bed. Lucas lounged against a pillow, watching her, sheet pulled up to midtorso, bisecting the trio of intriguing tribal circles tattooed along the left edge of his ribs.

His eyes were on fire.

He was so gorgeous, and he was all hers for the night. As many nights as she chose, apparently. A shiver shimmied up her back, part anticipation and part nerves.

"You want to know what tipped the scales?" she asked, arms crossed so it wasn't obvious her hands were shaking.

"More than I want to take my next breath."

She eyed the length of his body stretched out in the bed. "Ironically, that you were willing to sleep on the floor."

He laughed, and the vibration thrummed through her abdomen. "So you're saying I had you at hello?"

"No. I'm pretty sure you had me at Versace. It's painful to admit I was so easily bought with a designer gown." She said it flippantly, so he'd know she was kidding.

Except she wasn't, exactly. It was difficult to swallow how much she liked his gifts. What did that say about her?

"I'm glad one of us thinks this was easy. I've never worked so hard to get a woman into bed in my life."

"An unrecoverable blow to your ego, no doubt." She cocked her hip and jammed a hand down on it. Had she been so exhausted less than an hour ago that she could barely stand? Adrenaline and a hefty craving for Lucas coursed through her. "And it's so funny, but I'd swear I'm not actually in bed yet. Perhaps your work isn't done after all."

With a growl, he flung off the sheet, sprang up from the mattress and crawled toward her, completely, beautifully naked. Her mouth went dry.

Wickedness flashed through his expression, and the shiver

it unleashed in her this time was all anticipation. She absolutely could not mistake how much she turned him on.

This was all for her. Not for him. He'd said so, and she intended to hold him to it.

He rose up on his knees in front of her and extended a hand. She took it and braced to be yanked onto the bed. Instead, he held each finger to his lips and kissed them individually. By the time he reached the pinkie, he'd added licking and sucking and the rough texture of his tongue burned across her flesh.

He pressed her palm to his chest and left it there. Then, he cupped her face reverently. "Beautiful. So beautiful."

Before she could squawk out a lame "Thank you," he captured her mouth with his and held the kiss, lips suspended in time, and a tornado of need whirled through her womb.

Slowly, he angled his head and parted her mouth with his lips, and heat poured into her body. His tongue found hers, gliding forward and back in a sensuous dance.

Her nails dug into his rock-hard chest, scrabbling for purchase to keep her off the carpet. The kiss went on and on and stoked the flame of desire higher and higher in her belly.

Slow. It was all about slow with Lucas, and it was exquisite torture. She needed more, needed him now.

She broke away and reached for him, but he shook his head. His hands skimmed up her arms and down her back, came around to the front again, and both thumbs hooked the hem of her tank top. Gradually, he drew it skyward as he watched her from below half-closed lids.

"You're, um, not going to make me get in the bed?" she asked hoarsely.

"Nope." He pulled her top free from her raised arms and tossed it over his shoulder, and then he encircled her waist with an arm to draw her closer, his gaze ravenous as it traveled over her bare breasts. "You chose not to get in bed. I choose to take care of you right where you're at."

Her nipples rubbed his naked torso and beaded instantly and fire erupted in her womb, drawing a moan from deep in her throat. If he kept whispering that whiskey-smooth voice across her bare skin, it wouldn't take long to rip a verbally induced climax out of her. But she hoped for a hands-on approach.

He obliged her. One hand glided to the small of her back and pushed, jutting her breasts up and allowing him to capture a nipple with his tongue in a searing, swirling lasso.

She gripped his shoulders, lost in a slow spiral toward brainlessness as he sucked and laved at her sensitive flesh.

He switched sides and treated the other nipple to his magically delicious mouth. When he skated hard teeth across the peak, her legs buckled. Why hadn't she gotten in bed?

His hand delved inside her shorts, along her bare bottom. His fingers slipped into the crevice, lifting her and crushing her to his torso, supporting her.

The shock of Lucas touching her *there* had her gasping, but a solid pang of want swallowed the shock. *"Madre de Dios."*

Lucas groaned against her breast. With it still in his mouth, he mumbled, "I love it when you talk dirty."

A throaty laugh burst out of her. "It means mother of God, dingbat."

"I don't care. Anything you say in Spanish sounds dirty. Say something else." He licked his way down her stomach and bit the tie on her shorts, pulling the strings loose with his mouth.

"Quiero que ahora—"

And then her brain shut off when he yanked down her shorts and panties. He turned her and pressed her spine to his torso, settling her rear against his hard length. His firm arm snaked between her breasts, locking her in place, and his clever fingers slid down her stomach to find her center.

He mouthed her throat and rubbed the hard button between

her folds until she squirmed against the restraining band of steel disguised as his arm.

One finger slid inside and then two, in and out, and her head rolled against his shoulder in a mindless thrash. So good, so hot. So everything.

His heavy arousal burned into the soft flesh of her bottom, thrilling her. His thumb worked her nub in a circle and the sensuous onslaught swirled into one bright gathering point against his fingers. She came so hard she cried out.

The ripples tightened her inner walls around his fingers, and he plunged his fingers in again and again to draw out the climax to impossible lengths until, finally, it ended in a spectacular burst.

Lucas had just ruined her for any other man.

Too spent to stand on her own, she slumped in his arms and her knees gave out. The additional weight must have caught him off guard, and she pulled him down with her. In a tangle of limbs, they hit the carpet, and Lucas laughed as he rolled her back into his arms.

"There you have it," he said into her hair. "Now we don't have to lie. Next time someone asks why we got married, you can truthfully say we fell for each other."

A giggle slipped out and cleared the fog in her head, along with any lingering tension from being with Lucas, naked and exposed. His ability to bring the fun was unparalleled.

He picked her up and laid her gently on the bed.

"The first one is for you," he said, eyes crystal clear blue and dazzling. "The next one is for me."

"That's fair." She cleared her throat. He deserved more than she knew how to give him. "Lucas? I'm nowhere near as um…practiced at this as you are. However, I promise to give it my best shot."

She dragged an elbow under her to sit up but he knocked it away. She flopped back on the tangle of sheets and watched as he straddled her, powerful thighs preventing his gorgeous body from crushing her.

All of him was beautiful, but in this position, the really good stuff lay at eye level. She didn't hesitate to look her fill and reached out to run her palms along his legs. So hard and so delectable.

"No." He shook his head. "*Your* next orgasm is for me. The first one doesn't count. It's only to take the edge off, and, honey, you were wound tight. I barely touched you and you went off like a Roman candle."

She moaned. "That was a demonstration of 'barely'?"

With a wicked smile, he laced their fingers together and drew her arms up above her head, manacled her wrists together with one hand and slid the other hand down the length of her side from shoulder to hip. "Oh, yeah. There's much, much more. But this time, I get to pick where you'll be, and it'll be right here, where I can watch you."

He began to touch her, watching her as he did, and his heavy-lidded stare unnerved her, even as it heightened the sensations of his hands and mouth on her bare skin. He did something sinful to every inch of her body until she couldn't breathe with the need for him to fill her.

Why had she resisted a man with Lucas's skill for so long? There wasn't a whole lot of taking pleasure necessary when he gave it so freely. How selfish was she that she stingily lapped it up?

After what felt like hours of lovely agony, he settled between her legs and his talented mouth dipped to the place he'd pleasured with his fingers. With his lips and teeth and, oh, yes, his tongue working her flesh, he drove her into the heavens a second time.

His eyes never left her, and her shuddering release intensified with the knowledge that he was watching her, taking his own pleasure in hers. The manifestation of the power he spoke of, the power she held, was exhilarating.

"Enough," she gasped. "I admit it. You were right. I could have slept in my room, but I guess part of me wanted you to force the issue. So I could keep pretending I'm not attracted to you. No more pretending. I want you. Now."

"That might be the sweetest confession I've ever heard." He rose up over her and captured her mouth in way-too-short, musky kiss. "But we have all night. And tomorrow night. So, slow down, darlin'. Half the fun is getting there."

"How is it not making you insane to keep waiting your turn?"

He laughed and threaded his hands through her hair in a long caress. "Good things come to those who wait. Besides, I'm dead center in the middle of my turn. Every nuance of desire flashing through your eyes turns me on. Every moan from your mouth is like music. I could watch you shatter for hours."

Hours? *Dios.* She should have read between the lines a little better when he blew off the pregnancy issue back by the pool. "You, um, do plan to eventually get around to a more traditional version of sex. Right?"

"Oh, you better believe it, honey. Later."

Later. She loved later.

Sacrifice and selflessness had ruled her for so long, it felt incredible to let go. To let Lucas take care of her. To be greedy for once and wallow in pure sensation and pleasure instead of shoving aside her needs for fear everything she depended on would be taken away in an instant.

How freeing to have it all on the table and be given permission to just have fun.

For all his talk, Lucas almost lost it—again—during Cia's third climax.

She was beautiful, like Mozart at sunrise, and she was so sensitive, he set off the third one accidentally by blowing on her. She cried out his name and exploded, bowing up with that awesome arch to her back, and an answering pulse grew stronger in his gut.

He clamped his teeth down hard to keep his own release under control. His muscles strained, aching with the effort it took not to plow into her sweet, sweet center right then and there, no condom, just her and unbelievable satisfaction.

The battle stretched out for an eternity and, for a moment, he feared he'd do it. He rolled away and fixated on the oscillating ceiling fan above the bed, willing back the crush of lust.

This little fireball he'd married was not going to break his self-control. Never mind that he'd invented this game of multiple orgasms to demonstrate this was nothing but sex between two people who were hot for each other. To confirm that this insane attraction wasn't as strong as he'd imagined and that there was nothing special about this particular woman.

Somewhere along the way, the scent of Cia's arousal and the total surrender in her responses eliminated his intentions.

She fell back onto the pillow with a sexy sigh, lifting her breasts and making his mouth water. "You melted my bones that time. As soon as I can walk, I'm going to make you the best cup of coffee you've ever had in your life."

That pulled a chuckle out of him, though it hurt clear to his knees to laugh. "The benefits are good enough to reverse your stance on making a man coffee, huh?"

"I cannot believe there wasn't a picket line of your ex-lovers at the courthouse the day we got married."

Yeah, he knew a trick or two about pleasuring a woman, and his genuine enjoyment of it helped, but this was a far cry from how he normally went about it. Nothing about this affair with Cia remotely resembled how he normally interacted with a woman.

How did he explain that to her when he didn't get it, either?

"You're funny. There are more women who would be happy to read my obituary notice than would be upset I married you."

She snorted. "I doubt that. But as your wife, I believe I have the right to claim a few privileges."

If he breathed through his mouth, he couldn't smell her lotion anymore, and the lack eased the pain a tiny bit. "Yeah? Like what?"

"Like the right to say it's later."

Without another word, she flipped and crawled on top of him, sliding up the length of his body, hot as a lava flow, and whipping his crushing need into a frenetic firestorm.

Her eyes were so dark, they were almost black. They met his with thirst in their depths. The evidence of her desire lanced through his gut.

Her mouth fit to his, pulling on his lips and sucking his tongue forward. A guttural moan wrenched free from his throat, and she absorbed it into the heat of her kiss. He flung his arms around her and bound her to his chest, desperate to keep her in place.

The things this woman did to him. It defied description. Thankfully, she'd agreed to exorcise this wicked draw between them by acting on it instead of pretending it didn't exist.

Long dark hair fell into his face, trailing along his fevered skin, sensitizing it and begging for attention. He wound it up in a fist and guided her head to the side, lips following the line of her neck with fierce suction, laving her skin with his tongue, crazy with the craving to taste her.

Lime and coconut invaded his senses, both curse and cure, snaking through his head like a narcotic, heightening the wild lust.

Her body covered his, scalding breasts flat against his chest, her hands shoved in his hair, fingers sparking where she touched his scalp. One leg straddled him, opening her up. Her hips gyrated and tilted her center against his throbbing tip. Damp heat flared out, enveloping him, and his eyes glazed.

Now. The keening scream exploded in his head as she dragged her slick center up the length of his erection.

"Wait," he bit out, with no idea whether he was talking to her or his questing hips, which had a mind of their own.

He stretched out a hand to fumble with the drawer knob on the bedside table, shifting her center. Should have already had a foil packet under the pillow, top torn off. Fingers closed over the box and an eternity later, he unrolled the condom.

The second he was sheathed, Cia wiggled back into place atop him, nudged him once and impaled herself to the hilt with a feminine gasp.

His eyelids snapped shut as he filled her. His body shrieked to start pumping, but he forced himself to give her a minute to adjust.

Amazing. So tight. He pulsed as she stretched to accommodate him. Stretched perfectly, just enough, just right. Experimentally, she slid up and back down, rolling her pelvis, driving him home.

Home. A place for him. Only him.

He echoed her hip thrusts and heaviness built upon itself, spiraling higher and energizing him to move faster and faster.

"Lucas," she breathed. "I… Will you, um, look at me? I like it when you watch me."

He worked his lids open and greedily soaked in the visual perfection of the female form astride him. Why had his eyes been closed this whole time? The empowerment, the sheer magnificence, plastered across her face forced all the air from his lungs in a hard whoosh.

He'd done that for her. Unleashed her desire from its boundaries and allowed her free rein to take pleasure from his body, exactly as he'd insisted.

And she was taking it. Acknowledging it. Returning it tenfold. It was unbelievably hot.

Her torso undulated in a primal dance, nipples peaked and

firm atop alabaster breasts. She threw her head back, plunging him deeper, and long hair brushed his thighs.

Sparkling pressure radiated from his groin. Willing it back, he clamped a hand on her thigh, trying to slow her wanton thrusts, but she bucked against him and the tightness shoved him to the very edge.

He couldn't stop. He couldn't wait for her.

But then she came apart and the shock waves blasted down his length, triggering his release. Their simultaneous climaxes fed each other, like oxygen to a flame, dragging out the sensations and flooding his whole body with warmth.

Flooding his body with something else, something nameless and heavy and powerful.

With a sated moan, she collapsed against him, nestling into the hollow of his shoulder, and he gripped her close, absorbing every last bit of warmth, too lost in the lush, thick haze of Cia to move. They were still joined, and he basked in a thrilling sense of triumph.

Only with him could Cia be like this.

Now would be an excellent time to put distance between them. But he couldn't find the energy. Couldn't figure out why he wasn't all that interested in distance when he knew he should be. Never had sex been like that, a frantic and mindless rush toward completion.

Completion, not release. Even this—*especially* this—was bigger, stronger and more meaningful with Cia.

He'd proven something to himself, all right. Something earthshaking. Something fearsome. This wasn't casual sex between two people. He'd been making love to his wife.

Nine

In the morning, Cia woke half-buried under Lucas, and it made her smile. One heavy arm pinned her to his chest and his legs tangled with hers, trapping her bottom against his abdomen. His heat at predawn was delicious, warming her sore and stretched body.

It had been a while. Since college, back when she'd still been convinced the right man's love would heal her. All she'd done was prove sex didn't equal love, and both were ingredients in the recipe to misery.

If her high school days had resembled most red-blooded Americans', she might have figured out how to handle relationships then, instead of lumbering into her mid-twenties without a clue. Now she finally got it.

As long as she divorced sex from emotion and commitment, no problem. Divorce rocked.

She unscrambled their limbs without waking him and slipped out of bed to head for a much-needed hot shower. It probably wouldn't have taken any effort at all to nudge

Lucas into semiawareness and then take shameless advantage of him, but she was anxious to get to the shelter. A part of her hoped Pamela would still be there, but in her heart, she knew better. Regardless, the other women would need someone to talk to.

In no time, she dressed and tiptoed out of the bedroom she now shared with the sexy, slumbering man sprawled out across the bed. *Later,* she promised. No-strings-attached sex was the most awesome thing ever invented.

Pamela was indeed gone for good when Cia arrived at the shelter. The other women seemed dejected and upset. How self-centered was she for being in such a good mood, for shutting her eyes and savoring memories of the previous night? But she couldn't help it and had to force herself to stop humming three times while handling the most unexciting tasks.

Since she'd stayed so late the night before and arrived at seven that morning, Cia elected to leave at three.

She should be wiped out, but as she drove home, her mind got busy with one topic only—seeing Lucas again as soon as possible. She couldn't stop fantasizing about him. About the beyond-sexy trio of tattoos down the length of his torso and how she'd like to experiment on him a little to see how many times she could make him explode in a night.

Was it cool to call him and ask about his schedule? She'd almost sent him a text at least once every ten minutes, just to check in. Or say thanks for an awesome time last night. Or something else not so lame, but she had no idea about the rules when the person she was sleeping with was also her fake husband.

They'd done a lot of talking last night. But not once had Lucas mentioned what their relationship would look like going forward.

So frustrating. And ridiculous. It wasn't as if she could casually ask Courtney the requisite number of days to wait before calling when the guy involved was Cia's husband. As far as her friend knew, the marriage was still business only, and Cia wanted to get used to the change before admitting anything to anyone.

Besides, she and Lucas *still* weren't dating. Maybe it was okay to let her spouse know she was into him. In a strictly hot for his body kind of way.

Once at home, she stopped in the kitchen to get a glass of water and drank it while standing at the sink. Before she could swallow the second mouthful, said spouse blew through the door, startling her into dropping the glass into the sink.

"What are you doing home?" she asked.

Lucas strode toward her in a dark suit, which encased his shoulders with perfection, and a dark, impossible-to-misread expression on his face. Raw masculinity whipped through the kitchen to engulf her a moment before the man did.

He caught her in his arms and kissed her, openmouthed, hungrily, working her backward until her butt hit the countertop's edge.

She was trapped between hard granite and hard Lucas, and he was devouring her whole with his mouth. A whirlwind of desire kicked up in her center.

Dull thunks registered, and Lucas's hands delved inside her shirt, yanking down her bra and palming her breasts. Buttons. He'd popped all the buttons on her shirt and they'd thunked to the floor.

Four seconds later, he stripped her. Then he tore off his jacket, ripped the rest of his clothes half off and boosted her onto the counter. Cold stone cooled her bare bottom and sizzled against her fevered core.

Less than five minutes after he'd walked in the door, he spread her legs wide and plunged in with a heavy groan.

She dropped into the spiral of need and hooked her legs behind him, urging him on. His mouth was everywhere, hot and insatiable. His thrusts were hard, fast. She met him each time, already eager for the next one. Pinpoints of sensation swirled and then burst as she came, milking his climax.

What happened to *slow down?*

They slumped together, chests heaving, her head on his shoulder and his head on hers. She put her arms around him for support since her spine had been replaced with Jell-O.

"Um, hi," she said, without a trace of irony. If this was what their relationship would look like going forward, the view agreed with her quite well.

"Hi," he repeated, and she heard the smile in his voice.

"How was your day?"

He laughed and it rumbled against her abdomen. "Unproductive except for the last ten minutes. You distracted me all day. Don't disappear tomorrow morning. I'd like to wake up with you."

The explosive countertop sex had been hot, but the simplicity, the normalcy, of his request warmed her. "It's not my fault you're such a heavy sleeper. Set an alarm."

"Maybe I will." Carefully, he separated from her and trashed the condom. He helped her to the floor and gathered up her clothes, which he handed off, then began pulling on his own clothes with casual nonchalance. "I have another favor. I swear I was going to ask first but, darlin', you have to stop looking at me like that when I come in."

When his muscled, inked torso disappeared behind his ruined shirt, she sighed. Those tribal tattoos symbolized Lucas to a T—untamed, unexpected and thoroughly hidden beneath the surface. One of his many layers few people were aware existed, let alone privileged enough to experience. How lucky was she?

"You looked at me first." Of course, he always looked at her like a chocoholic with unlimited credit at the door of a sweetshop. "What's the favor? Do I get another dress out of the deal?"

He grinned and kissed her hand. "Of course. Except this time, I intend to take it off of you afterward."

"Or during." She shrugged and opted to toss her irreparable blouse in the trash. Lucas might end up buying her a new wardrobe after all, by default. "You know, if it's boring and you happen to spy a coat closet or whatever."

His irises flared with heat and zinged her right in the abdomen. "Why, Mrs. Wheeler, that is indeed a fine offer. I will surely keep it under advisement. Come with me and let's see about your dress."

Mrs. Wheeler. He'd called her that before, and it was her official title, so it shouldn't lodge in her windpipe, cutting off her air supply.

But it did. Maybe because she'd just been the recipient of a mind-blowing climax courtesy of Mr. Wheeler.

He took her hand and led her upstairs, where the couture fairies had left a garment bag hanging over her closet door. Her fake husband was a man of many, many talents, and she appreciated every last one.

"By the way," Lucas said. "When I ran into the maid earlier, I told her we'd had a little misunderstanding about a former girlfriend, but you were noble enough to get past it. I hope that's okay. Any excuse for why we weren't sharing a bedroom is better than nothing, right?"

"More than okay. Perfect." And not just the excuse. While she still basked in the afterglow of amazing sex, everything about Lucas was perfect.

The deep blue dress matched her eyes and eclipsed the red one in style and fit. Lucas leaned against the doorjamb of the bathroom, watching her dress with a crystalline focus and making complimentary noises. His attention made her feel beautiful and desired, two things she'd never expected to like.

Lucas Wheeler was a master of filling gaps, not creating them. Of giving, not taking. Ironic how she'd accused him of being selfish when trying to convince him to marry her.

As they entered the Calliope Foundation Charity Ball, a cluster of Wheelers surrounded them. Lucas's parents, she already knew, but she met his grandparents for the first time and couldn't help but contrast the open, smiling couple to Abuelo's tendency to be remote.

Matthew joined them amid the hellos, and his cool smile reminded her she owed Lucas one asset of a wife. It was the very least she could do in return for his selflessness over the entire course of their acquaintance.

A room full of society folk and money and lots of opportunities to put her foot in her mouth were nearly last on her list of fun activities, right after cleaning toilets and oral surgery. But she kept her hand in Lucas's as they worked the room; she laughed at his jokes, smiled at the men he spoke to and complimented their wives' jewelry or dress.

There had to be more, a way to do something more tangible than tittering over lame golf stories and smiling through a fifteen-minute discourse on the Rangers' bull pen.

"Are these clients or potential clients?" she asked Lucas after several rounds of social niceties and a very short dance with Grandfather Wheeler because she couldn't say *no* when he asked so nicely.

"Mostly potential. As I'm sure you're aware, our client list is rather sparse at the moment."

"Is there someone you're targeting?"

"Moore. He still hasn't signed. Matthew invited another potential, who's up here from Houston. George Walsh. He's looking to expand, and if I'm not mistaken, he just walked in."

If Walsh lived elsewhere, the Lana fiasco probably factored little in his decision process. "Industry?"

"Concrete. Pipes, foundations, that sort of thing. He's looking for an existing facility with the potential to convert but wouldn't be opposed to build-to-suit." He laughed and shook his head. "You can't be interested in all this."

"But I am. Or I wouldn't have asked. Introduce me to this Walsh."

With an assessing once-over, he nodded, then led her to where Matthew conversed with a fortyish man in an ill-fitting suit.

Matthew performed the introductions, and Cia automatically evaluated George Walsh. A working man with calluses, who ran his company personally and preferred to get his hands dirty in the day to day. Now what?

Schmoozing felt so fake, and she'd never been good at it. Lucas managed to be genuine, so maybe her attitude was the problem. How could she get better?

Though it sliced through her with a serrated edge, she shut her eyes for a brief second and channeled her mother in a social setting. What would she have done? Drinks. Graciousness. Smiles. Then business.

Cia asked Walsh his drink preference and signaled a waiter as she chatted about his family, his hobbies and his last vacation. Smiling brightly, she called up every shred of business acumen in her brain. "So, Mr. Walsh, talk to me about the concrete business. This is certainly a booming area. Every new building needs a concrete foundation, right?"

He lit up and talked for a solid ten minutes about the weather, the economy and a hundred other reasons to set up shop in north Texas. Periodically, she threw in comments about Lucas and his commitment to clients—which in no way counted as fabrication since she had firsthand experience with his thoughtful consideration and careful attention to details.

Somehow, the conversation became more than acting as an asset to Lucas and enhancing his reputation, more than reciprocation for upholding his end of the bargain. She'd failed at drumming up donations for the shelter, despite believing in it so deeply. Here, she was a part of a partnership, one half of Mr. and Mrs. Wheeler, and that profoundly changed her ability to succeed.

It reiterated that this marriage was her best shot at fulfilling her mother's wishes.

"Did I do okay?" she whispered to Lucas after Matthew took Walsh off to meet some other people.

Instead of answering, he backed her into a secluded corner, behind a potted palm, and pulled her into his arms. Then he kissed her with shameless heat.

Helplessly, she clung to his strong shoulders as he explored every corner of her mouth. His strength and solid build gave him the means to do the only thing he claimed to want—to take care of her. It wasn't as horrible or overbearing as she might have anticipated.

It was…nice. He understood her, what she wanted. Her dreams. Her fears. And they were partners. Who had amazing sex.

When he pulled back, the smile on his face took her breath.

"More than okay," he said. "Are you angling to join the firm?"

"Well, my name *is* Wheeler," she said in jest, but it didn't seem as funny out loud. That was a whole different kind of partnership. Permanent. Real. Not part of the plan.

"Yes. It is." He lifted her chin to pierce her with a charged look. The ballroom's lighting refracted inside his eyes, brightening them. He leaned in, and the world shrank down to encompass only the two of them as he laid his lips on hers in a tender kiss. A kiss with none of the heat and none of the carnal passion sizzling between them like the first time.

It was a lover's kiss. Her limp hands hung at her sides as her heart squeezed.

Oh, no. No, no, no.

"We have to find that coat closet. Now," she hissed against his mouth. Sex. That's all there was between them, all she'd allow. No tenderness, no affection, no stupid, girlie heart quivers.

His eyebrows flew up. "Now? We just got he— Why am I arguing about this?"

Linking hands, he pulled her along at a brisk trot, and she almost laughed at the intensity of his search for a private room. Around a corner of the hotel's long hallway, they found an empty storage room.

Lucas held the door and shooed her in, slammed it shut and backed her against the wood, his ravenous mouth on hers.

The world righted itself as the hard press of his body heated hers through the deep blue dress. This, she accepted. Two people slaking a mutual wild thirst and nothing more.

"Condom," she whispered.

He had about four seconds to produce it. An accidental pregnancy would tie her to this man for life, and, besides, she didn't want children. Well, she didn't want to cause herself heartache, which was practically the same thing.

"Right here. I was warned I'd need it."

Fabric bunched around her waist an instant later, and her panties hit the ground. He lifted her effortlessly, squashing her against the door and spreading her legs, wrapping them around him.

The second he entered her—buried so deep, every pulse of his hard length nudging her womb—she threw her head back and rode the wave to a mind-draining climax.

Yes. Brainless and blistering. Perfect.

When she came down and met the glowing eyes of her husband, a charged, momentous crackle passed between them.

She'd keep right on pretending she hadn't noticed.

Warm sunlight poured through the window of Lucas's office. He swiveled his chair away from it and forced his attention back to the sales contract on his laptop screen. Property—dirt, buildings, concrete or any combination—lived in his DNA and he'd dedicated his entire adulthood to it. It shouldn't be so difficult to concentrate on his lifeblood.

It was.

His imagination seemed bent on inventing ways to get out of the office and go home. In the past few weeks, he'd met a sprinkler repairman, an attic radiant barrier consultant and a decorator. A *decorator*. Flimsy, he had to admit.

A couple of times after showings, he'd swung by the house, which was mostly on the way back to the office. Through absolutely no fault of his own, Cia had been home all those times, as well, and it would have been a crime against nature not to take advantage of the totally coincidental timing.

Ironic how a marriage created to rescue his business was the very thing stealing his attention from business.

Moore had signed. Walsh had signed. Both men were enthusiastic about the purchases they'd committed to, and Lucas intended to ensure they stayed that way. Cia's interactions with them had been the clincher; he was convinced.

His dad had gone out of his way to tell Lucas how good this marriage was for him, how happy he seemed. And why wouldn't he be? Cia was amazing, and he got to wake up with her long hair tangled in his fingers every morning.

The past few weeks had been the best of his life. The next few could be even better as long as he kept ignoring how Cia had bled into his everyday existence. Every time they made love, the hooks dug in a little deeper. Her shadows rarely appeared now, and he enjoyed keeping them away for her. He liked that she needed him.

If he ignored it all, it wasn't really happening.

Matthew knocked on the open door, his frame taut and face blank. "Dad called. Grandpa's in the hospital," he said. "Heart attack. It's not good. Dad wants us to come and sit with Mama."

Heart attack? Not Grandpa. That heavy weight settled back into place on his chest, a weight that hadn't been there since the night he met Cia.

Lucas rose on unsteady legs. "What? No way. Grandpa's

healthier than you and me put together. He beat me at golf a month ago."

Protesting. Like it would change facts. His grandfather was a vibrant man. Seventy-five years old, sure, but he kept his finger on the pulse of Texas real estate and still acted as a full partner in the firm.

When Lucas had graduated from college, Grandpa had handed him an envelope with the papers granting Lucas a quarter ownership in Wheeler Family Partners. A careworn copy lined the inner pocket of his workbag and always would.

"I'll drive." Matthew turned and stalked away without waiting for Lucas.

Lucas threw his laptop in his bag and shouldered it, then texted Helena to reschedule his appointments for the day as he walked out. Once seated in Matthew's SUV, he texted Cia. His wife would be expected at the hospital.

The Cityplace building loomed on the right as Matthew drove north out of downtown. They didn't talk. They never talked anymore except about work or baseball. But nothing of substance, by Matthew's choice.

They'd been indivisible before Amber. She'd come along, and Matthew had happily become half of a couple. Lucas observed from a distance with respect and maybe a small amount of envy. Of course his relationship with Matthew had shifted, as it should, but then Amber died and his brother disappeared entirely.

Lucas sat with his family in the waiting room, tapped out a few emails on his phone and exchanged strained small talk with Mama. His dad paced and barked at hospital personnel until a dour doctor appeared with the bad news.

Lucas watched his dad embrace Mama, and she sobbed on his shirt. In that moment, they were not his parents, but two people who turned to each other, for richer or poorer, in sickness and in health.

Apart from everyone, Matthew haunted the window, stoic

and unyielding as always, refusing to engage or share his misery with anyone. Not even Lucas.

The scene unfolded in surreal, grinding slow motion. He couldn't process the idea of his grandfather, the Wheeler patriarch, being gone.

Cia, her long, shiny hair flying, barreled into the waiting room and straight into Lucas. He flung his arms around her small body in a fierce clinch.

The premise that she'd come solely for the sake of appearances vanished. She was here. His wife was in his arms, right where she should be. The world settled. He clutched her tight, and coconut and lime wafted into his senses, breaking open the weight on his chest.

Now it was real. Now it was final. Grandpa was gone, and he hadn't gotten to say goodbye.

"I'm glad you came," Lucas said, and his voice hitched. "He didn't make it."

"I'm sorry, so sorry. He was a great man," she murmured into his shirt, warm hands sliding along his back, and they stood there for forever while he fought for control over the devastating grief.

When he tilted his head to rest a cheek on top of Cia's hair, he caught Matthew watching them, arms crossed, with an odd expression on his face. Missing his own wife most likely.

Finally, Lucas let Cia slip from his embrace. She gripped his hand and followed silently as he spoke to his dad, then she drove him to his parents' house with careful attention to the speed limit.

Mama talked about funeral arrangements with his father and grandmother, and through it all Cia never left his side, offering quiet support and an occasional comforting squeeze. Surely she had other commitments, other things she'd rather be doing than hanging out in a place where everyone spoke in hushed tones about death.

Her keys remained in her purse, untouched, and she didn't leave.

It meant a lot that she cared enough to stay. It said a lot, too—they'd become friends as well as lovers. He hadn't expected that. He'd never had that.

For the first time, he considered what might happen after the divorce. Would they still have contact? Could they maintain some kind of relationship, maybe a friends-with-benefits deal?

He pondered the sudden idea until Matthew motioned him outside. Cia buzzed around the kitchen fixing Mama a drink, so he followed his brother out to the screened-in porch.

Matthew retrieved a longneck from a small refrigerator tucked into the corner, popped the top with the tail of his button-down in a practiced twist and flopped into a wicker chair, swigging heartily from the bottle.

Lucas started to comment about the hour, but a beer with his brother on the afternoon of his grandfather's death didn't sound half-bad. Might cure his dry throat.

Bottle in hand, Lucas took the opposite chair and swung one leg over the arm. "Long day."

Matthew swallowed. "Long life. Gets longer every day."

"That's depressing." His life got better every day, and considering the disaster it had been, that was saying something. Lucas hesitated but plunged ahead. "Do you want to talk about it?"

"No. But I have to." He sighed. "First Amber. Now Grandpa. I'm done. It's the last straw. I can't take it anymore."

That sounded serious. Suicidal even. Lucas looked at his normally solid and secure brother. "Do you need a vacation?"

"Yeah." Matthew laughed sarcastically. "From myself. Problem is they don't offer that with an all-inclusive resort package. I don't know what it's going to take to get me back on track, but whatever it is, it's not here."

"Where is it?"

Shrugging, Matthew drained his beer in record time. "I

have no idea. But I have to look for it. So I'm leaving. Not just for a few days. Permanently."

"Permanently?" Lucas shook his head. Matthew was a Wheeler. Wheelers didn't take off and let the chips fall. Everything Lucas knew about being a Wheeler he'd learned from watching his brother succeed at whatever he attempted. Obviously Matthew was overtired. "You can't leave. Take some time away. You've been working too much, which is my fault. Let me handle clients for a week or two. Backpack through the Himalayas or drink margaritas in Belize. But you have to come back."

"No, I don't. I can't." Stubborn to the core. That was one Wheeler trait they shared.

"Wheeler Family Partners isn't a one-man show. We just lost Grandpa. Dad's been taking a backseat for a couple of years, and now he's going to be the executor for Grandpa's estate. We're it."

And Matthew was more it than Lucas-the-gray-sheep could ever be.

Matthew's sharp gaze roved over Lucas in assessment. "You can do it without me. You've changed in the past year. Maybe Lana snapped some sense into you, or maybe it started happening long before and I didn't see it. Regardless, you've turned into me."

"Turned into you? What does that mean?"

"Responsible. Married. Committed. I always thought I'd be the one to settle down, have a family. Raise the next generation of Wheelers to carry on WFP. But lo and behold, it's not going to be me. It's going to be you."

The beer bottle slipped out of Lucas's hand and broke in two against the concrete patterned patio. The sharp yeasty scent of the last third of a beer split the air. "What are you talking about? I'm not settling down. There's no family in my future."

"Right." His brother snorted. "If Cia's not pregnant within a month, I'll fall over in a dead shock."

Oh, man. They'd done a spectacular job of fooling everyone into believing this was the real thing, and now Matthew felt safe leaving the firm in Lucas's hands. "Uh, we're being careful. She's not interested in having children."

"Yeah, well, accidents happen. Especially as many times as I'd bet you're doing it. You're not quite as subtle as you must think when you dash off during an event and sneak back in later, without giving Cia a chance to comb her hair. You two are so smoking hot for each other, I can't believe you haven't set something on fire."

So now he was supposed to apologize for enjoying sex with his wife? "Sorry if that bothers you," Lucas retorted. "We have a normal, healthy relationship. What's the problem?"

Matthew raised his brows. "No problem. Why so defensive? I'm pointing out that you landed on your feet. That's great. I'm happy for you. I admit, I thought you rushed into this marriage because of Lana or, at the very least, because you'd screwed up and gotten a one-night stand pregnant. Clearly, I was wrong. Cia's good for you. You obviously love each other very much."

He and Cia surely deserved Oscars if Matthew, who missed nothing, believed that. "Thanks."

"Although," Matthew continued in his big-brother tone, "you probably should have thought twice about marrying someone who doesn't want kids. Isn't family important to you?"

If the marriage had been intended to last, he definitely would have thought more about it back on that terrace. Now Matthew's words crowded his mind, shoving everything else out. "Isn't it important to *you?* You're the one talking about abandoning everyone."

"Only because you can take my place. You can be me and

I can be you. I'll go find fun and meaningless experiences, without worrying about anything other than myself."

"Hey now." Was that how his brother saw him? "Lay off the cheap shots."

"Sorry." Matthew gave him an assessing once-over. "Six months ago, you wouldn't have blinked at such a comment. It's an interesting transposition we have going on. You have no idea how hard it is for me to think about marrying again. Having a baby with someone who isn't Amber. Something is busted inside, which can't be repaired. Ever."

Quiet desperation filled Matthew's voice, the kind Lucas would never have associated with his older brother, who had always looked out for him. Whom Lucas had always looked up to, ever since the first time Matthew had stood shoulder to shoulder with his little brother against bullies. As Matthew took full responsibility for a broken flowerpot because he hadn't taught Lucas the proper way to hold a bat. As Matthew passed off the first client to his newly graduated brother and whispered the steps to Lucas behind the scenes.

A long surge unsettled Lucas's stomach. His brother had never been so open, so broken.

Matthew needed him. The firm, his family, his heritage all needed him. Lucas had to step up and prove his brother's faith in him wasn't misplaced. To show everyone Lucas knew what it meant to be a Wheeler, once and for all.

It would be hard, and parts of it would suck. But he had to.

Of course, he lacked a wife who wanted all the ties of a permanent marriage or who looked forward to filling a nursery with blankets and diapers. Where in the world would he find someone he liked as much as Cia, who excited him like she did even when they were nowhere near a bed? It would take a miracle to tick off all the points on his future-wife mental checklist. A miracle to find a wife as good as Cia.

Matthew clamped his mouth into a thin line and shifted his attention as Cia's hand slid across Lucas's shoulder.

"I didn't mean to interrupt," she said. "I just wanted to check on you. Doing okay?"

Concern carved a furrow between her brows, and he didn't like being the cause of that line. "Fine, darlin'. Thanks."

"Okay. I'm going to sit with your mom for a little while longer. She's pretty upset." She smiled and bent to kiss the top of his head, as if they were a real married couple in the middle of for better or worse.

His vision tunneled as future and present collided, and a radical idea popped fully formed into his head. An idea as provocative and intriguing as it was dangerous. One that would pose the greatest challenge thus far in his relationship with Cia.

What if they didn't get divorced?

Ten

A noise woke Cia in the middle of the night. No, not a noise, but a sixth sense of the atmosphere changing. Lucas. He'd finally pried himself loose from his laptop and paperwork. His study might be in the same house, but it might as well have been in Timbuktu for all she'd seen of him lately.

She glanced at the clock—1:00 a.m.—as he slid into bed and gathered her up against his warm, scrumptious body, spooning them together.

"Sorry," he whispered. "Time got away from me."

"It's okay. You're earlier than last night." And the night before that and the night before that. In the weeks since his grandfather's death and Matthew's disappearance, he'd been tense and preoccupied, but closemouthed about it other than to say he'd been working a lot.

She rolled in his arms and glued her body to his, silently offering whatever he wanted to take, because he'd done the same when she'd needed it. Sometimes he held her close and dropped into a dead sleep. Sometimes he was keyed up and wanted to talk. Sometimes he watched TV, which she always left on for him despite her hatred of the pulsing lights.

Tonight, he flipped off the TV and covered her mouth in a searing kiss. His hands skimmed down her back to cup her bottom, sliding into the places craving his careful attention.

Oh, yes. Her favorite of the late-night options—slow, achingly sensual and delicious. The kind of night where they whispered to each other in the dark and pleasured by touch, lost inside a world where nothing else existed.

In the dark, she didn't have to worry about what hidden depths of the heart might spring into her eyes. No agonizing over whether something similar crept through his eyes, as well. Or didn't. It was better to leave certain aspects of their relationship unexamined.

Of course, ignoring the facts didn't magically rearrange them into a new version of truth.

The truth was still the truth.

This was more than just sex.

Sex could be fun, but it didn't erase the significance of doing it with Lucas. Not some random, fun guy. *Lucas,* who got out of the way and let her make her own choices. Lucas, who'd proven over and over he was more than enough man to handle whatever she threw at him.

When the earth stopped quaking, Lucas bound her to him in a tight tangle of limbs. He murmured, *"Mi amante,"* and fell asleep with his lips against her temple.

When had he managed to squeeze in a Spanish lesson? His layers were endless and each one weighed a little more, sinking a little deeper into her soul.

This thing with Lucas was spiraling out of control. They were still getting a divorce, and all this *significance*—and how much she wanted it—freaked her out. It would be smart to back off now, so it wouldn't be so hard later.

In the morning, she woke sinfully late, still nestled in Lucas's arms for the first time in a long time, and she didn't hesitate to test how heavily he slept. The exact opposite of backing off. *Stupid* was her middle name lately.

"Mmm. Darlin', that is indeed a nice way to wake up," he murmured, after she'd sated them both.

"Stay in bed tomorrow morning, and you might get a repeat." She flipped on the TV and settled in to watch the weather while contemplating breakfast. "Can you eat or are you going to go drown yourself in listings right away?"

"I'm taking a little personal time this morning. I deserve it, don't you think?"

"Yeah. Does that mean I'm breakfast?"

He laughed. "Yep. Then I want to take you somewhere."

But he wouldn't tell her where until after they'd eaten, showered and dressed, and he'd driven to a run-down building miles off the freeway in an older part of town full of senior centers and assisted-living facilities.

"This just came up for sale," he told her as he helped her out of the car and led her to the edge of the parking lot. "It's an old hotel."

She glanced at him and back at the building. "I'm sorry. I'm not following why we're here or what the implication of this is."

"For the shelter," Lucas said quietly. "It can be retrofitted, and I checked on the zoning. No problems."

"The shelter." It took another thirty seconds for his meaning to sink in. "You mean my shelter? I'm planning to have it built."

"I know. This is another option. A less expensive option. Thirty-five percent down and I know a few people we can talk to about the financing."

"Financing?" If he'd started speaking Swahili, she'd have been equally as challenged to keep up. "I'm not getting a loan. That's the whole point of accessing my trust fund, so I can pay cash and the shelter will never be threatened with closure. We went over this. Without the trust money, I don't have thirty-five percent, let alone enough to purchase."

He clasped her hand with painstaking care. "I'll give you the money for the down payment."

The air grew heavy and ominous, tightening her chest. Their agreement specifically called for their assets to remain separate, and that might prove to be a touchier subject than sex. "You didn't get a terminal cancer diagnosis or something, did you? What's this all about?"

"You inspire me. Your commitment to victims of abuse is amazing. If I help you do this, you could start the shelter now instead of waiting until you get your money when the divorce is final. Save a few more women in the meantime."

"Oh, Lucas."

And that was it. Her heart did a pirouette and splattered somewhere in the vicinity of her stomach.

She rushed on, determined not to dwell on how many king's horses and how many king's men it would take to put everything back together again. "I appreciate what you're saying—I really do. But I can't get a loan, not for the kind of money we're talking about. I told you, Courtney and I tried. Our business plan wasn't viable, and venture capitalists want profits. Asking you to marry me was the absolute last resort, but it turned out for the best. If we have a loan, there's always a possibility of foreclosure if donations dry up, and I can't have that hanging over our heads."

No bank would ever own her shelter. Nothing would have the power to rip it from her fingers. It was far, far better to do it all on her own and never depend on anyone else. Much less painful that way.

"Okay. So, no loan." A strange light appeared in his eyes. "At least think about the possibility of this place. The owner is motivated to sell. Adding in the renovations, the purchase price is around a third of the cost to build. You could save millions."

Yes, she could. The savings could be rolled forward into operating costs, and it would be years and years before she needed to worry about additional funds beyond the trust money. The idea had merit. She could run the shelter without donations, a huge plus in her mind.

Maybe Lucas could talk the owner into waiting to sell until the divorce came through and she had access to the trust.

She surveyed the site again. The hotel was tucked away in a heavily treed area, off the beaten path. Bad for a hotel and good for a shelter the victims didn't want their abusers to find. "I do like the location. It's important for women who've taken the step to leave their abusers to feel safe. An out-of-the-way place is ideal. Tell me more about your thoughts."

Lucas started talking, his voice wandering along her spine, the same way his hands did when he reached for her at night. He threw around real estate terms and an impressive amount of research. When he was all professional and authoritative about his area of expertise, it pulled at her and bobbled her focus, which wasn't so sharp right now anyway.

Her brain was too busy arguing with her heart about whether she'd actually been stupid enough to fall for her all-too-real husband.

No question about it. She'd put herself in exactly the position she'd sworn never to be in again—reliant on a man to make her complete and happy. All her internal assurances to the contrary and all the pretending had been lies.

This was where brainless had gotten her: harboring impossible feelings for Lucas.

It hardly mattered if Lucas freed her to jump in and enjoy life alongside him. It hardly mattered if she'd accidentally married a man who understood her and everything she was about. It hardly mattered if she wished her soul had room for a mate and that such fairy tales existed.

They didn't.

Life didn't allow for such simplicity. Anything she valued

was subject to being taken away, and the tighter she held on, the greater the hurt when it was gone. The only way to stay whole was to beat fate to the punch by getting rid of it first.

She'd married Lucas Wheeler because he wasn't capable of more than short-term. She could trust him to keep his word and grant her a divorce, the sole outcome she could accept.

They had a deal, not a future.

Midway through an email, Lucas realized it had been four days since he'd spent time with his wife outside of bed. Their time together in bed had been less than leisurely and far from ideal. It was criminal.

He picked up the phone. "Helena. Can you reschedule everything after five today?"

"I can," she said. "But your five-thirty is with Mr. Moore and it's the only day this week he can meet. The counteroffer was a mess, remember?"

He remembered. Once upon a time, he would have passed it off to Matthew and dashed for the door. The deficiency created by his brother's vanishing act multiplied every day, demanding one hundred percent of his energy and motivation, leaving none for Cia.

He missed her. "Reschedule everything else, then. Thanks—you're the best."

If he put aside a potential new client's proposal, skipped lunch and called in a couple of favors, he'd have an infallible amended contract ready to go by five-thirty and a happy Moore out the door by six. Dinner with Cia by seven.

The challenge got his blood pumping. The tightrope grew thinner and the balancing act more delicate, but without his brother to fall back on, new strengths appeared daily.

He was thriving, like Matthew had predicted, because every night Lucas went to bed with the ultimate example of sacrifice and commitment. He and Cia were partners. How could he look in the mirror if he didn't step up?

He texted Cia with the dinner invitation, and her response put a smile on his face for the rest of the day: It's a date.

A date with his wife. The wife he secretly contemplated keeping. *Forever* didn't fill him with dread or have him looking for the exit. Yet. He'd been nursing the idea in the back of his mind, weighing it out. Testing it for feasibility. Working the angles. If he didn't file for divorce, he'd have to give up Manzanares because he hadn't fulfilled his end of the bargain.

There was a lot to consider, especially the effort required to convince Cia to look at their agreement in a different light.

It was time to take the next step and see how difficult Cia would be about staying married. The six months were more than half over, and he had a suspicion it would take a while to bring her around, even with the added incentive of his idea of using the hotel for the shelter.

Moore agreed to the amended contract and walked out the door at five forty-five, giving Lucas plenty of time to cook a spectacular dinner for Cia. The poolside venue beat a restaurant by a country mile, and the summer heat wasn't unbearable yet.

They sat at the patio table and exchanged light stories about their day as a breeze teased Cia's hair. He waited until dessert to broach the main topic on his mind. "Have you thought any further about the hotel site?"

Her eyes lit up. "That's all I've thought about. Courtney and I have been redoing the numbers, and she's excited about it. I'm pretty sure I'm going to buy it. It was a great idea, and I appreciate all the work you put into it." She hesitated for a beat and met his gaze. "Would it be weird to ask you to be my broker if we're in the middle of a divorce?"

Perfect segue. "About that. You can't wait until you get your trust fund to buy. There are other interested parties already. A bank loan is out, I realize, but I can scrape up the money. Would you accept it?"

She stared at him. "The entire purchase price, plus renovation costs? Not just the thirty-five percent down? Lucas, that's millions of dollars. You'd be willing to do that for me?"

Yeah, he knew the offer was substantial. What he hadn't realized until this moment was that his high level of motivation at work hadn't been solely to prove something to himself and to Matthew. The more successful he could make WFP now, the less of a blow it would be to lose Manzanares, which was a given if he convinced her to forget about the divorce.

"Not as a loan. In trade."

"Trade? I don't have anything worth that much except my trust fund."

"You do. You."

"We're already married. It's not like you have a shot at some sort of indecent proposal," she said with a half laugh.

What he had in mind was a thoroughly decent proposal. "I'm curious. What do you think of this house?"

"Could you veer between subjects any faster?" Her eyes widened. "Oh, you were seriously asking? I love this house. It'll be hard to go back home to my tiny Uptown condo after living here. Why, are we about to be kicked out?"

"Before Matthew left, he sold it to me."

"This is *Matthew's* house? Shocking how that hasn't come up before." She waved it away before he could formulate a response. "But I'm not shocked you bought it. It's beautiful, and I'm sure you'll be happy here for a long time."

It hadn't come up before because it hadn't been important. When she'd first proposed this deal, the house represented a place to live, which he had been able to access quickly and easily, and it had provided a good foundation for their fake relationship.

Now, as he sat at the patio table with his wife, eating dinner in a house he owned, it represented a potential future. A real future. One where he could fulfill the expectations that came with being a Wheeler.

"Actually…" He traced a line across the back of Cia's hand

and then threw every last card and a whole second deck on the table. "I'd like for you to be happy here, too. Married to me. Long-term."

The sip of wine she'd taken sprayed all over the flagstone patio. "That wasn't funny."

"It wasn't a joke. We're partners, and we're amazing together. Why ruin a good thing with a divorce?"

"Why?" Fire shot from her expression and singed the atmosphere. "Why? Because we *agreed*. If you don't file for divorce, I can't access my trust fund and I'll tear up the Manzanares contract. We both have a huge stake in this."

Interesting how her argument summarized the deal instead of listing the evils of marriage. He shrugged. "But the divorce isn't necessary if I give you the money for the shelter."

She sprang to her feet and both palms slammed the table, rattling the dishes. "Are you sure you have a business degree, Wheeler? You're forgetting about a minor detail called operating expenses. Without the trust fund, I won't have a dime once we open the doors. The residents have to eat. There are administrative costs. Utilities."

Like that, they were back to *Wheeler* and insults. And logic. No, he hadn't considered the operating expenses because his involvement in any deal ended the moment papers were signed. Poor excuse, regardless, and a huge miss. It had been much easier to coax her into his bed.

He blew out a frustrated breath. "What if we could get donations for operating expenses? Would you still want a divorce?"

Her eyes flared wide, deepening the blue. "What have you been drinking, Wheeler? Our whole agreement centers on the divorce."

Okay. He'd botched this up. Clearly. He'd opted to go with money as his negotiation instrument and had ignored what he'd learned about Cia over the past few months.

Figure it out, or lose everything.

Pulse tripping with a rush of sudden alarm, he rose and cornered her against the table. The heat between them, the absolute beauty and inexpressible pleasure of making love—that was his best bargaining tool, his best shot at getting her to stay.

Her arms came up and latched into a knot across her chest. She was not budging an inch.

"Darlin'," he said and slid a hand through her curtain of hair to cup the back of her silky neck. "I've been drunk on you since the moment you said I look like a Ken doll. Loosen up a little. We're just talking."

The rigid set of her shoulders and the corded neck muscles under his fingers were the opposite of loose and getting tighter by the moment. "Talking about how you're second-guessing our divorce."

He leaned in and set his lips on her forehead, mouthing his way down to her ear. "Not second-guessing. Presenting a possible alternative. Can you blame me? Honey, the things you do to me are indeed mind-blowing. I'd be a few cows shy of a herd if I was willing to give that up so easily."

His hands found her breasts, and she moaned. "Animal analogies. That's sexy, Wheeler. Talk to me some more like that." Her arms unknotted and fell to her sides, melting into pliancy as he sucked on her throat. She didn't move away.

"You like that? How about this?" He backhanded the dishes to the ground, and amid the crash of breaking pottery, set her on the table, splaying her legs wide to accommodate his hips. Her dress bunched at her thighs and hot pink flashed from the vicinity of her center. "You make me crazier than a monkey on fermented melons. Hotter than a rattler on asphalt. Shall I go on?"

"No. No more animals."

She was laughing, and he captured it in his mouth, then parted her lips and tasted the wine lingering inside with firm strokes of his tongue. She arched against him, rubbing her heat against his blistering erection.

He worked a hand under her bottom and pushed, grinding that heat hard against his length. "You feel that?" he growled. "That's what you do to me. I want to be inside you every minute of every day. I want your gorgeous naked body under me, thrashing with climax, and my name on your lips. I cannot get enough of you."

Her body spasmed, and she moaned again, her chest vibrating against his. He pulled her dress over her head and feasted on the sight of one very sexy hot-pink bra and panty combo.

It needed to come off now. He needed to touch her.

With one finger, he hooked her bra and dragged it down across her taut nipples, popping them free. He took one in his mouth, rolling it across his tongue, nibbling and sucking, and she pushed against his teeth, begging him to take her deeper.

He sucked harder. Her nails bit into the back of his head, urging him on. His erection pulsed, aching to be free of the confines of his clothes.

Not yet.

He dragged his tongue down the length of her abdomen and fingered off her panties, then knelt between her legs to pleasure her there.

"Do you like this?" he asked. "Do you like the way I make you feel?" He treated her to a thorough openmouthed French kiss square in the heart of her wet heat. She bucked against his lips, seeking more.

"Yes. *Yes.*"

She was so responsive, so hot. Fingers deep inside her, he flicked her sweet nub with his tongue. "What do you need?"

She whimpered, writhing as he held back from granting her the release she sought. "You, Lucas," she said on a long sob. "I need you."

The syllables uncurled inside him, settling with heavy, warm weight, and only then did he realize how much he'd burned to hear them. He vaulted to his feet. His clothes hit the patio, and he had a condom in his hand in record time.

His luscious wife watched him with dark, stormy eyes, one leg dangling over the edge and one leg bent up, opening her secrets wide. A wanton gift, spread out on the table, just for him.

He kissed her, covering her mouth and her body simultaneously, then entered her with a groan, filling her, and squeezed his eyes shut to savor the hot, slick pressure.

They were awesome together. How could she deny it? How could she walk away? No other man could fulfill her like he could.

She needed him.

She only thought she wasn't in the market for a long-term marriage, like she'd once insisted she didn't want him like this. She was wrong, so wrong, about both, and he had to convince her of it.

Relentlessly, he drove her off the edge and followed her down a brilliant slide toward the light.

Later, when Cia lay snuggled in his arms in their bed, she blasted him with the last word. "The divorce is happening, no matter how hot the sex is. I asked you to marry me because you're a close-the-deal-and-move-on guy. Stop talking crazy and do what you're good at."

Yeah, he excelled at moving on. Always on the lookout for the next deal, the next woman, the next indulgence. Matthew was the solid, responsible one.

Was. Not anymore.

Lucas pulled Cia tighter into his arms without responding. Matthew was gone. Lucas had assumed his place at the helm of Wheeler Family Partners. Lucas owned a house constructed for marriage. With these shifts, life could be whatever he wanted.

He wanted what Matthew had lost. With Cia. For the first time in his life, Lucas wasn't interested in moving on. But how did he convince Cia to stick around? Maybe she was right and he wasn't cut out for long-term. Gray sheep didn't spontaneously turn white overnight.

But the shifts had already occurred, and he didn't have to stay on the same path. This was it, right here, right now. If he wanted to change the future, he had to figure out how to make it happen.

Eleven

When the doorbell chimed, Fran Wheeler was the very last person Cia expected to view through the peephole. She yanked open the door and summoned a smile for her mother-in-law. "Mrs. Wheeler. Please come in."

"I'm sorry to drop by unexpectedly." Fran stepped into the foyer, murmuring appreciatively at the way Cia had decorated the living room. "And please, call me Fran. Formality makes me feel old, and if I wanted to be reminded of my age, I'd look in a mirror."

"Of course. Fran, then. Lucas isn't home, I'm afraid." Cia waved at the couch. "Would you like a seat? I'd be happy to get you a drink while you wait, if you'd like."

Coolly, as only a pillar of Dallas society could, Fran cocked her head, and the chic style of her blond hair stayed firmly in place. "I'm here to see you. Lucas is with his father at a boring real estate seminar, so I took a chance you'd be home alone."

Uh-oh. Well, she was way overdue for the tongue-lashing Fran likely wanted to give her for refusing the pearls. "Your timing is good, then. I took the day off from work. The offer of a drink still stands."

A squawk cut her off. Fergie couldn't stand it when someone had a conversation without her.

Fran glanced toward the back of the house. "Was that a bird?"

"A parrot." Another squawk, louder and more insistent. "Fergie. She was a wedding present from Lucas."

"Oh." Fran's raised brows indicated her clear interest, but she appeared reluctant to ask any further questions.

Cia's fault, no doubt, as she had no idea how to break the awkward tension. The divorce loomed on the horizon. She was sleeping with this woman's son. The mechanics of a relationship with a mother figure escaped her. The odds of successfully navigating this surprise visit were about the same as winning the lottery without buying a ticket.

Squawk.

"Fergie probably wants to meet you." Cia shook her head. "I mean, she's a little temperamental and likes people around. If you're not opposed to it, we can sit in the kitchen. She'll quiet down if we do."

"That's fine." Fran followed Cia into the kitchen and immediately crossed to Fergie's cage. "Oh, she's precious. Does she talk?"

"When she feels like it. Say hello to her. Sometimes that works."

Cia poured two glasses of iced tea.

Fran and Fergie exchanged hellos several times, and Fergie went off on a tangent, first singing the national anthem and then squawking, "Play ball!" to the older woman's delight. Fran laughed and praised the bird for a good five minutes. Cia wasn't about to interrupt.

Finally, Fran joined Cia at the breakfast table and sipped her tea. "The last few weeks have been difficult, and I wanted to thank you for the shoulder. It meant a lot to me that you stayed with us the afternoon Andy's father died and then all through the funeral and…" She took a deep breath. "Well, you know, you were there. So thanks."

"Oh, um, you're welcome." Cia's tongue felt too big for her mouth, swollen by the sincerity of Fran's tremulous smile. "I know how it feels to lose a parent. I was glad to do what I could."

"You're very good for Lucas—did you know that? Andy says you're all he talks about at work. My boys are everything to me, and I'm grateful Lucas has found someone who makes him happy." The older woman reached out and clasped Cia's hand. "We got off on the wrong foot when I pushed too soon for a relationship with you, but I'm hopeful we can start over now."

Cia shut her eyes for a blink. What was she supposed to do? She wasn't just sleeping with Lucas; they were married. And it wasn't over yet. Abuelo could still get suspicious if Fran happened to mention Cia's aloof brush-offs. Dallas was a small town in all the worst ways.

"Fran, you aren't to blame. It's me." Might as well lay it all out there. "I just don't know how to be around a mother-in-law. Or a mother, for that matter."

Okay, she hadn't meant to lay it *all* out there. Tears stabbed at her eyelids, and Fran's expression softened.

"There aren't any rules, honey. Let's just sit here, drink tea and talk. That's all I want."

Yeah, she could pretend all day long this was about keeping the heat off and guarding against her grandfather's suspicions. It wasn't. Fran was offering something she couldn't refuse—friendship.

Cia nodded and cleared her throat. "That sounds nice. What would you like to talk about?"

"Tell me about the shelter. I've been looking for a volunteer opportunity. Can I help?"

And for the second time in less than a week, Cia's heart

splattered into a big, mushy mess. A man she could get over in time. A mother? Not so much. And now it was too late to back away.

With her nerves screaming in protest, Cia told Fran every detail about the shelter and how she'd picked up where her mother left off. Silently, she bargained with herself, insisting the cause could use a good champion like Fran Wheeler and evaluating the possibility of still working with her after the divorce.

But she knew Fran wouldn't speak to her again after Lucas divorced her. That was better anyway. A clean break from both mother and son would be easier.

Way back in the far corner of Cia's mind, a worm of suspicion gained some teeth. What if Lucas had put his mother up to coming by in some weird, twisted ploy to get her to reconsider the divorce?

No, he wouldn't do that. She pushed the doubt away.

Lucas was honest about everything, and he hadn't mentioned staying married again anyway, thank goodness. For a second after he'd casually thrown out *long-term,* her pulse had shuddered to a halt and her suddenly active imagination had come up with all sorts of reasons why it could work. All pure fiction.

His suggestion had been nothing but an off-the-cuff idea, which he hadn't been serious about in the first place. Exactly why she was ignoring all the feelings Lucas had churned up when they'd stood outside the old hotel—she'd be gutted if she gave him the slightest opening.

Besides, there was no *alternative* to divorce. The trust clause stated she couldn't file for divorce. He had to.

As she ushered Fran to the door with the promise of meeting her for lunch next Monday, Cia had herself convinced she and Lucas were on the same page about the divorce.

* * *

The green dress Lucas bought Cia for the Friends of the Dallas Museum of Art benefit gala was her favorite. Sheer silk brushed her skin like a cloud, and the neckline transformed her small breasts, giving her a bit of cleavage. She'd twisted her hair into an updo and a few rebel tendrils fell around her face. Sexy, if she did say so herself.

Lucas, criminally stunning in an Armani tux, came into the bathroom as she stepped into her black sandals. He swept her hand to his lips and zapped heat straight through her tummy.

The man had touched her as intimately as possible, in more ways than she'd imagined existed. Yet a simple kiss on the back of her hand turned her knees to jelly.

"Mrs. Wheeler, you are indeed ravishing." He pulled a flat box from the pocket of his jacket. Without taking his eyes off her, he opened the lid and offered her the box.

Cia glanced inside and her already weak knees almost pitched her to the travertine tile.

"Lucas," she squeaked, and that was the extent of her throat's ability to make sound.

He extracted the necklace and guided her to the mirror, then stood behind her to clasp the choker around her neck. Emeralds set in delicate filigreed platinum spilled over her collarbone, flashing fire and ice against her skin. Every eye would be drawn to the dazzling piece of art around her neck, and no one would even notice her cleavage.

"It reminds me of you," he murmured in her ear, not touching her at all, but his heat, a signature she recognized the moment he walked into a room, raced up her bare back. "An inferno captured inside a beautiful shell. All those hard edges polished away to reveal a treasure. Do you like it?"

Did she *like* it? That was akin to asking if she liked the sun or breathing. The necklace wasn't jewelry, the way every other man on earth gave women jewelry. It was a metaphor for how well he understood her.

Lucas had an uncanny ability to peer into her soul and pluck out her essential desires, then present them to her.

Similar to his mother's pearls, this necklace represented all the frightening, unexamined things in her heart, which Lucas never let her forget. Neither could she forget he'd very pointedly failed to mention the things in *his* heart.

"I can't keep it." Her hand flew to the clasp, only to be stilled by his.

"Yes. You can. I insist."

"It's too..." Personal. Meaningful. Complicated. "Expensive. I'm sure you still have the receipt. Take it back."

"The artist custom-made it for you. All sales are final."

She shut her eyes for a beat. "That's not the kind of thing you do for a woman you're about to divorce. How are we going to make it look like we're on the outs if you're buying me custom-made jewelry?"

They had time, but they'd done such a bang-up job of making a fake marriage look real, reversing it presented a whole new set of difficulties. She wished she'd considered that before hopping into Lucas's bed.

"Maybe I'm trying to earn your forgiveness," he suggested, and in the mirror, his gaze locked on hers, a blue firestorm winding around her, daring her to ask what he'd done that required forgiveness.

Was this an apology for bringing up an *alternative* to divorce? "Forgiveness for an affair, maybe? You wouldn't do that."

His forehead tightened. "How do you know what I'm capable of?"

She spun away from the mirror, about to remind him that he'd been the one to convince her he'd never cheat. His black expression changed her mind. "Because I do. Only someone with a huge ego and a heaping spoonful of selfish has an affair. You don't have the qualifications."

They stared at each other for the longest time, and, finally, Lucas blinked, clearing his expression, and gave her a slow smile. "So maybe I'm trying to earn your forgiveness for slaving away at the office. Leaving you alone for days on end, crying into your pillow about how your husband never pays attention to you anymore."

"That could work," she said, then squealed as he backed her up against the vanity and slid magic fingertips up her leg, gathering green silk against his wrist.

"It's been so long, hasn't it, darlin'? Are you desperate for my hands on you? Like this?" His palm flattened against her bottom and inched under her panties, stealing her breath as he dipped into her instantly wet center.

Yes, exactly like that.

"We have to leave or we'll be late," she choked out and squirmed against his wicked fingers. "Rain check. You and me and a coat closet. Nine o'clock. We'll pretend it's the first time we've been able to connect in weeks."

With his eyes blazing, he hooked the edge of her panties and drew them off to puddle on the floor. "How about we connect right now *and* I meet you in the coat closet? But only if you make it eight-thirty and leave your underwear at home."

As if she could resist him. Within moments, he'd sheathed himself and they joined, beautifully and completely.

She clung to him, wrapped her legs around him and plunged into pleasure. Pleasure with an edge because her brain had left the building, and he'd ended up with a piece of her heart after all. She couldn't find the courage to shut off what she was feeling.

When Lucas made love to her, she forgot all the reasons why the *alternative* wasn't plausible. Lucas glided home slowly, watching her with a searing, heavy expression, and her heart asked, "What if it could be?"

The question echoed with no answer.

No answer, because Lucas was *not* presenting an alternative to divorce so they could continue having spectacular sex, no matter what he claimed.

Sex wasn't the basis for a relationship. Sex wasn't guaranteed to stay good, let alone spectacular. He hadn't miraculously fallen in love with her. So why had he really brought up long-term?

And why was she so sad? Because his alternative hadn't included a declaration from his heart or because it felt as though she didn't know the whole truth?

It didn't matter. This time she wouldn't end up brokenhearted and disillusioned because she wasn't giving Lucas the chance to do either.

They arrived at the benefit twenty minutes late, and it would have been thirty if Lucas hadn't tipped the driver to speed. Regardless, heads swiveled as they entered the ballroom, and Cia struggled not to duck behind Lucas.

"What are they looking at?" she whispered. "I told you there was no such thing as fashionably late."

"Maybe they know you're not wearing any panties," he said, a lot more loudly than she would have liked, and made her skin sizzle with a sinful leer.

She smacked his arm with her clutch. "Maybe they know you stuffed them in your pocket."

The swish of fabric alerted her to someone else's presence. Lucas's mother. She stood right in front of them, and as far as Cia knew, still possessed working ears. Cia's smile died as heat climbed across her face.

"Lovely to see you, Mrs. Wheeler," Cia croaked. The fire in her face sparked higher. "I'm sorry, I mean Fran. You'd think it would be easy to remember. I don't like being called Mrs. Wheeler, either. Makes me feel like an impostor."

Where had that come from? She sealed her lips together before more stupid comments fell out, though dragging her son's sex life into public had probably already killed any warm feelings her mother-in-law might have developed over afternoon tea.

The older woman's cheeks were a little pink, but she cleared her throat and said, "No problem. I couldn't answer to it for at least a year after Andy and I married. Such a big change in identity. Wait until you have kids and they start calling you 'Mama.' That one's worse, yet so much more wonderful."

Another couple joined them, and Cia was caught up in introductions instead of being forced to come up with a neutral response to Fran's casually thrown out comment. It didn't stop the notion from ricocheting through her head.

Kids. No, thank you.

Lucas's warm hand settled at the small of her back as he talked shop to the couple who had asked Fran for an introduction. The wife needed larger office space for her CPA business. Cia smiled and nodded and pretended as though she wasn't imagining how Lucas would approach fatherhood.

But she was.

He'd kiss her pregnant belly while peering up at her through those clear blue eyes. He'd treat her reverently, fetching her drinks and rubbing her feet.

When the baby cried at night, he'd smooth Cia's hair back and tell her to stay in bed while he handled it. Later, he'd throw a ball for hours with a little dark-haired toddler. Lucas would label it fun and insist work could wait, even if it couldn't.

As quickly as those wispy images materialized, they vanished in favor of much clearer images of flashing lights atop black-and-white squad cars and grim-faced policemen who knocked on the door in the middle of the night to utter the words, "I'm sorry. The accident was fatal. Your parents are gone."

The only way she could guarantee that no child of hers

would ever go through that was not to have any children. She tucked away the sudden, jagged longing for a life that would never be.

Fran's friends wandered toward the dance floor, the wife clutching the business card Lucas had retrieved from a hard, silver case, and another well-dressed couple looking for a real estate broker promptly replaced them.

"This is my wife, Cia Wheeler," Lucas said.

"Robert Graves," the male half of the couple said and shook Cia's hand. "Formerly Allende, right?"

"Right. Benicio Allende is my grandfather."

Robert's eyes grew a touch warmer. "I thought so. My company does the advertising for Manzanares. It keeps us hopping."

"Oh?" Cia asked politely.

It never ceased to amaze her how people loved to name-drop and rub elbows because of her last name. *Former* last name. Robert Graves was no exception, prattling on about Abuelo's shrewd negotiations and then switching gears to announce right then and there that he'd like to do business with Lucas. It wasn't said, but it was clearly implied that he'd decided because of her.

She made Lucas stable. Connected. Exactly as they'd hoped this marriage would do.

The room spun. Was that why Lucas wanted to blow off the divorce? Because he didn't need the Manzanares contract to save his business anymore but he did need her?

Not possible. A few paltry clients couldn't compare to the coup of Manzanares. She'd done exhaustive research. She'd considered all the angles.

Except for the one where she worked hard to be an asset to her husband and succeeded.

No. He'd keep his word. He had a high ethical standard. Surely he'd return to form before too long. Lucas excelled at racing off to the next woman—his brother had even warned her of it.

Lucas didn't want to give up sex. Fine. Neither did she, and *compromise* wasn't a foreign word in her vocabulary. They could keep seeing each other on the sly after the divorce.

The idea loosened the clench of her stomach. She didn't have to quit Lucas cold turkey, and, as a bonus, she would gain a little extra time to shut off all these unwelcome feelings she'd been fighting.

As soon as the Graves couple coasted out of earshot, Fran signaled a waiter, and Andy Wheeler joined the group in time to take a champagne flute from the gilded tray.

"A toast," Lucas's dad suggested with a raised glass. "To all the new developments and those yet to be born."

Cia raised her glass and took a healthy swallow.

"Oh, you're drinking," Fran said with obvious disappointment. "I guess there's no news yet."

Lucas flashed a wolfish smile in Cia's direction. "You'll be the second to know, Mama."

"Why do I feel like you're talking in code?" Cia whispered to Lucas.

"I might have casually mentioned we're trying to get pregnant," Lucas whispered back. "Don't worry. It's just window dressing."

"Window dressing?" Cia said at normal volume, too startled to rein in her voice. "What kind of window dressing is that?"

"Excuse us for a moment, please." Lucas nodded at his parents and dragged Cia away by the waist to an unpopulated corner of the room.

"Pregnant? Really?" she hissed and blinked against the scarlet haze over her vision. "No wonder your mom stopped by for tea and chatted me up about identity and being called 'Mama.'"

"Well, now. I guess I don't have to ask you how you feel

about the idea." Lucas tucked a tendril of hair behind her ear, and it took supreme will not to slap his hand away.

"It doesn't matter. We don't have a 'trying to get pregnant' marriage and never will. Should I say it again? In Spanish, maybe?" She stuck a finger deep into his ribs. "Why did you tell your parents something so ridiculous? We don't need any more window dressing. In fact, we should be taking the dressing *off* the window."

"Since several people are at this very moment watching us argue, I believe dressing is peeling away rapidly with every finger jab," Lucas responded. "Simmer down, darlin'. Matthew's gone. I'm the only Wheeler who has a reasonable shot at producing the next generation. It's Wheeler Family Partners. Remember?"

She swallowed, hard, and it scraped down her throat as if she'd gargled with razor blades. "So I'm supposed to be the factory for the Wheeler baby production? Is that the idea?"

"Shocking how people leap to cast my wife in that role. One might wonder why you're having a meltdown about the mere contemplation of bearing my children, when you've been so clear about how our marriage is fake and we're divorcing, period, end of story." He stared her down with raised eyebrows. "Mama was upset when Matthew left, and I told her we were trying for a baby to soften the blow. Not because I have some evil scheme to start poking holes in the condoms. Okay?"

Oh, God. All part of the show.

She filled her lungs for what felt like the first time in an hour and let the breath out slowly, along with all the blistering anger at Lucas for…whatever offenses she'd imagined. It was a lot to balance, with the sudden presentation of *alternatives* and being an asset and baby talk.

Evil scheme aside, Lucas still had a serious obligation to start a family, and he'd never shun it. Her lungs constricted again. They'd have to be extremely careful about birth control going forward.

Going forward? There wasn't much forward left in their relationship, and she stood in the way of his obligations. It would be selfish to keep seeing him after the divorce.

She grimaced at the thought of another woman falling all over herself to be the new Mrs. Wheeler. Cooing over his babies. Sleeping in his bed. Wearing his ring.

Soon, she'd be Señorita Allende again. That should have cheered her up. It didn't. "We could have easily coordinated stories. Why didn't you tell me earlier?"

Lucas lifted one shoulder and glanced at his Rolex. "Slipped my mind. It's almost eight-thirty. I'll race you to the coat closet."

She crossed her arms over another pang in her chest. "It's seven-fifteen, Wheeler. What is going on with you? As slippery as your mind is, you did not forget casually mentioning we're trying to get pregnant. You wanted to see my reaction in a place where I couldn't claw your skin off. Didn't you?"

A smear of guilt flashed through his eyes. He covered it, but not quickly enough to keep her stomach from turning over.

She was right. Oh, God, she was *right*.

Long-term marriage suddenly didn't seem like an off-the-cuff, not-really-serious suggestion. The anger she'd worked so hard to dismiss swept through her cheeks again, enflaming them.

"Not at all," he said smoothly. "I have a lot of balls in the air. Bound to drop one occasionally."

"Learn to juggle better or a couple of those balls will hit the ground so hard, I guarantee you'll never have children with anyone." She whirled to put some distance between them before she got started on that guarantee right this minute.

Lucas followed her back into the mix of people, wisely opting to let her stew instead of trying to offer some lame apology or, worse, throwing out an additional denial. Matthew's exodus had triggered more changes than the obvious ones.

Lucas's commitment phobia had withered up and died and now he'd started hacking away at hers with a dull machete. How could this night be any more of a disaster?

Fifteen minutes later, she found out exactly how much more of a disaster it could become when she overheard a conversation between four middle-aged men with the distinct smell of money wafting off them. They were blithely discussing her shelter.

She listened in horror, frozen in place behind them, as they loaded up plates at the buffet with shrimp and caviar, oblivious to the fact that they were discussing *her shelter.*

"Excellent visibility for the donors," one said, and another nodded.

Donors? Maybe she'd misheard the first part of the conversation. Maybe they weren't talking about the hotel site or her new shelter. They couldn't be. She'd made it very clear to Lucas she didn't want to depend on donations to run the shelter. Hadn't she?

"Any venture tied to Allende is a gold mine," the third declared. "How could you not be in after Wheeler's fantastic sales pitch? The property's in great shape. Most of the updating will be cosmetic, and the renovation contract is already on my lawyer's desk."

The property? Lucas had taken people to the site? How many people?

"Domestic violence is a little, shall we say, uncouth?" the fourth one suggested with a laugh. "But the Hispanic community is a worthwhile demographic to tap from a charitable perspective. It'll cinch my bid for mayor. That's the kind of thing voters want on your résumé."

Acid scalded her stomach. No. She hadn't misheard. Lucas had charged ahead without her—without her permission or even her knowledge. He'd made the proposed shelter site public, rendering it useless.

What more had Lucas done? Had he been presenting an *alternative* to divorce or a done deal?

What exactly had the necklace been an apology for?

Twelve

Lucas and Cia had been home a good twenty minutes and she hadn't spoken yet. In the car, she'd blasted him with a tirade about an overheard conversation, which she'd taken out of context, and then went mute. That alone chilled his skin, but coupled with the frosty set of her expression, even a stiff drink didn't melt the ice forming along his spine. So he had another.

Then he went looking for her.

The little ball in the center of the mattress was quiet, so he eased onto the edge of the bed. "I didn't know they were going to make such a big deal out of it."

Nothing.

He tried again. "Talk to me, honey. Scream at me. I don't care, as long as you don't keep up this deep freeze. This is all a big misunderstanding. I can fix it."

"Fix it?" The lethal whip of her tone sank into his skull, which was already sloshy with alcohol and the beginnings of a headache. She sat up, and the light from the bedside lamp cast half of her scrubbed face in shadow. "You've done enough fixing for today, Machiavelli. I'm tired. Go away and sleep somewhere else."

"Ouch. I'm in that much trouble?" He grinned, and she didn't return it. So, jokes weren't the way to go. Noted. "Come on, darlin'. I messed up. I shouldn't have taken people to the site. I'll find another hotel for your shelter if that site's compromised. It's not worth getting so upset over."

"Do I seem upset?" She stared at him, and her dry eyes bothered him more than the silent treatment. Unease snaked through his gut.

"No." He'd wandered into the middle of uncharted territory full of quicksand. This had all the trappings of their first official fight as a couple. Except they weren't really a couple—yet—and, technically, they argued all the time. "Does that mean you've already forgiven me?"

She palmed her forehead and squeezed. "You really don't get any of this, do you?"

"Yeah, I get it." Somehow, his plan to come up with the operating expenses for the shelter hadn't happened as envisioned. "You're ticked because I tried to tap sponsors for the shelter site, and now the location is compromised. I'm in real estate, darlin'. I'll find another one. A better one."

"I'm sure you will. Eventually." She lay back down and covered her head with an arm, blocking his view of her face. His firecracker's fuse was noticeably fizzled. How could they get past this if she wouldn't yell at him?

"Cia." He waited until she peeked out from below the crook of her elbow. "I should have talked to you before talking to the money. I'm sorry. Let's kiss and make up now, okay?"

"No. No more kissing. This isn't only about the shelter." Her voice was steady, a monotone with no hint of the fire or passion she normally directed at him. "It's about you running the show. You say I have a choice, but only if it's a choice you agree with. I'm not doing this anymore. In the morning, I'm moving back into my condo."

"What? You can't." This situation was unraveling faster than he could put it back together. But whatever happened, he couldn't let her leave. He wiped damp palms on the comforter and went with reason. "We have a deal. Six months."

The arm came off her face, and bitter laughter cut through the quiet bedroom. "A deal, Wheeler? We have a *deal?* Oh, that's rich. We have a deal when it's convenient for you to remember it. Every other waking moment, you're trying to alter the deal. Presenting alternatives. Trying to give me money. Talking about babies with your mother and seducing me into believing you really understand me. It's all about the deal, isn't it? As long as it's the best deal for *you.* What about what I want?"

He swore. Some of her points could be considered valid when viewed from a slightly different perspective. But her perspective was wrong—the tweaks to the deal were good for everyone. "What do you want?"

"A divorce! The same thing I've wanted since day one. I fail to understand how or when that fact became confusing to you."

"It's not confusing." He refused to lose control of the conversation. She needed him, and his job was to help her realize it. "I know that's what you think you want. But it's not."

"Oh, well, everything is so clear now. Are you aware of the fact that you talk in circles most of the time? Or is it deliberate, to bewilder your opponent into giving up?"

"Here's some straight talk for you. We're good together. We have fun, and I like being with you. You're fascinating, compelling, inspiring and all of that is out of bed. In bed…" He whistled. "Amazing. Beyond compare. I've told you this. No circles then. No circles now. Why can't you see a divorce is not what you need?"

"Do you hear yourself?" she asked so softly he strained

to pick up the words. "Your whole argument was about why a divorce is not what *you* need. My needs are foreign to you. And you've spent the last few months fooling me into believing the opposite, with the dresses and taking care of me and pretending you were interested in the shelter because you wanted to help me."

"I *do* want to help you," he snapped. God Almighty, she pushed his limits. Stubborn as a stripped screw. He forced his tone back into the realm of agreeable before he gave away the fact that she'd gotten to him. "You're mad because it was mutually beneficial? That's what made the original deal so attractive. We both got value out of it. Why is it so bad to continue the tradition?"

"All lies! Matthew left and now you're hot for a wife who'll give you a baby. You're too lazy to go find one, so you thought, 'Hey, I already have a wife. I'll hang on to her.'"

Lazy? She was more work than a roomful of spoiled debutantes and jaded supermodels. Yet there was not one woman he'd want long-term besides Cia. They were compatible on every level, and the thought of living his life without her—well, it wasn't a picture he liked. Why else would he be talking about it? "I get the feeling anything I say at this point would be wrong."

"Now you're onto something. There's no defense for any of it, least of all compromising the shelter site. If a woman's abuser finds the shelter, he might kill her. Do you understand how horrible your cavalier attitude is? Do you have any clue how it made me feel when I realized what those men were talking about?"

"I'm sorry. I do understand how important discretion is. It was a mistake. But I stand by my offer to find another site."

"How magnanimous of you," she said with a sneer. "I'm not stupid, Wheeler. You got me all excited about it, then oh, no. Bring in the entire upper crust of Dallas, so everyone knows where the shelter is. Oops. You sabotaged that site, hoping to buy time to talk me out of the divorce. Maybe *accidentally* get pregnant in the meantime."

Was she listening to anything he had said? He'd apologized twice already. "Compromising the site might have been the result but that was not my inten—"

"Betrayed. That's how I felt when I stood there listening to my entire world crumble around me."

Everything with Cia was a hundred times more effort than it needed to be, which he knew good and well she did on purpose to keep everyone at bay. But why was she still doing it with him? Hadn't they gotten past this point already? "That's a little melodramatic, don't you think?"

There came a tear, finally, sliding down her cheek. "Melodramatic? You broke my heart, Lucas!"

"What?" Every organ in his chest ground to a halt, and he couldn't tear his eyes away from the lone tear laden with despair and hurt.

No. No way. This marriage was about the benefits, both physically and business-wise. She needed his unique contribution to the relationship. Period.

He'd been one hundred percent certain she was on board with that. Hurt and feelings and messiness weren't part of the deal. And when the deal fell apart, he walked away. Usually.

But he was still here.

She dashed away the teardrop, but several more replaced it. "Surprised me, too."

All of this was too fast. Too much to process. "Whoa. What are you saying?"

"Same thing I've been saying. Since you have to file for the divorce, I have no power here. Therefore, I'm leaving, and I have to trust you'll eventually find another potential mother for your next generation, at which point I'll get my divorce. Clear enough for you?"

"No." He shook his head. "Back up, honey. Now *you're*

talking in circles. I didn't make you mad—I hurt you. How did that happen?"

"Because I'm an idiot." Her eyes shone with more unshed tears. "I had expectations of you that you couldn't fulfill. You're not the man I thought you were."

"Wait a minute. What did you expect?" He was still reeling from the discovery she'd developed *feelings* for him and hadn't bothered to say anything.

What would he have done with such information? Run in the other direction? Run faster toward her?

Actually, he didn't know what to do with it now.

"I expected you to be honest, not hide your real agenda." She snorted. "*Dios,* how naive am I? I walked right into it, eyes wide open, certain I could hang on to my soul since you weren't asking for it. You gave and gave, and I never saw it for what it was. An exchange. You slipped under my guard, and the whole time, you were planning to exact payment. You betrayed me, not once but twice, with alternatives and then with sponsors. You don't get a third chance to screw me over."

When thunderclouds gathered across Lucas's face, Cia was too tired to care that she'd finally cracked his composure.

"That's enough," Lucas declared. "I listened to your mental origami, and let me tell you, I am impressed with your ability to fold facts into a brand-new shape. But it's my turn to talk. Are you in love with me?"

She almost groaned. Why did he have to go there? "That's irrelevant."

He tipped her chin up and pierced her with those blue laser beams. Scared of what he'd see, she jerked away and buried her face in the pillow.

Great. The entire bed smelled of pine trees mixed with her lotion.

"It's not irrelevant to me," he countered quietly. "I'd like to know what's going on inside you."

So would she. Thoughts of babies and long-term should not be so hard to shove away. The hurt shouldn't be so sharp.

"Why?" she mumbled, her face still in the pillow.

He growled in obvious frustration, "Because I care about you."

She rolled over and said, "You have a funny way of showing it."

"Really? I'd argue the exact opposite."

"You can argue about it all day long. But you'd be wrong. You like to take care of me. That's different than caring about me."

He snapped out a derisive laugh. "Maybe we should start this whole conversation over. We suck at communicating unless it's 'more,' 'faster' or 'again,' don't we?"

No, they didn't have any communication problems when they were naked, which was exactly what had gotten her into this mess. Intimacy with Lucas could never be divorced from emotion. Why had she pretended it could be? "Which is why we're done with that part of our relationship."

He sighed. "Look, honey. I messed up. But I'm here, talking to you, trying to fix it. And you still never answered the question. Are you in love with me?"

"Stop asking me!" she burst out, determined to cut off his earnestness and dogged determination to uncover the secret longings of her heart that she didn't understand and did not want to share. He had enough power over her already. "It's just warm feelings for the man I'm sleeping with because he's superawesome in bed, okay? It doesn't change anything. You're not in love with me. You're still on the lookout for a baby factory. And I need a divorce, not all of these complications."

"Complications are challenges you haven't conquered yet," he said, and the tension in his face and shoulders visibly eased.

Her tension went through the roof.

Of course he hadn't fallen all over himself to declare his undying love. Not that she had expected him to after she'd backtracked about her broken heart.

In matters of the heart, they were cut from the same cloth—excellent at emotional distance and not much else. The divorce deal was perfect for them both.

"I'm not up for any more complications *or* challenges, thanks. Can we cut to the chase?" She sat up and faced him. "Are you going to file for divorce or not?"

He held her gaze without blinking, without giving away his thoughts. "No."

Her eyelids snapped closed. He'd finally made his move. *Checkmate.* "You can't do this to me, Lucas. Please."

"I can't do what? Give you what you really need instead of a divorce you'll regret? You're a vibrant, beautiful woman, yet you aim to shrivel up alone for the rest of your life. That's not right."

He ran a hand through her hair, letting it waterfall off his fingers, and his touch, so familiar, nearly caved in her stomach.

Being alone had never been her goal. Avoidance of suffering had been the intent, but she'd done a shoddy job of it, hadn't she? The tsunami of agony hadn't just drowned her; it had broken through every solid barrier inside, allowing sharp-edged secret dreams to flow out, drawing blood as they went.

"Cia, I'm offering a long-term partnership, with advantages for both of us. We already know we like each other. The sex is great. We'll figure out how to do your shelter without the trust fund. Together, we're unstoppable. Why can't you consider it?"

"Because it's not enough. There's a reason why I'll be alone for the rest of my life. I don't know how to do long-term." He started to respond, but she cut him off. "And neither do you. Sex isn't enough. Liking each other isn't enough."

He hurled out a curse. "What is enough?"

Love.

Oh, God. She wanted something he couldn't give her. Something she didn't know how to give him. No wonder she couldn't answer his questions.

She shied away from relationships because she had no idea how to love a man when living in constant fear of the pain and loss sure to follow. She had no idea how to love without becoming dangerously dependent on it.

Her parents had been in love. Until Lucas, she hadn't remembered all the long glances and hand-holding. The accident had overshadowed the history of their lives before that one shattering, defining moment. If they had lived, would she be having an entirely different conversation about the magic ingredients of a long-term relationship?

Would she better understand her own heart and demand Lucas know his?

"I can't tell you," she said. "You have to figure it out on your own."

He pressed the back of his neck with stiff fingers. "Fantastic. An impossible puzzle with no correct answer. Why can't this be about what looks good on paper?"

Sacar los ojos a uno. He was bleeding her white.

"It's all about how things look with you." She should have seen that before. Appearances were everything because skin-deep was all he permitted. Nothing could penetrate the armor he kept over his heart. "As long as it looks like fun, you're on board, right?"

"That's not fair. I never said a long-term marriage would be a big party. I don't know what it'll look like, but I do know I don't want what we have to be over." Gently he gripped her shoulders, and for a moment raw tenderness welled in his eyes. It made her pulse stutter and wrenched a tendril of hope from inside her. But then he said, "And I know you need what I bring to this relationship. You need me."

"No." She looked straight at him as her heart broke anew.

His entire offer hinged on dependency, the certainty that she was willing to be dependent. Not because he wanted to be with her. "Need is dangerous. It creates reliance. Addiction. Suddenly, you can't survive without the thing you crave. What happens when it's gone? I don't need selfishness disguised as partnership. I don't need someone who doesn't understand me. I don't need you, Lucas. Let me go."

Pain flashed across his face. Finally. This conversation had gone on for far too long. She'd run out of arguments, ways to get him out of the room before she went completely insane and begged him to figure out how to give her what she wanted.

"Yeah," he said and cleared his throat. "Okay. It's for the best."

As he slid off the bed and gathered some clothes from the dresser, she twisted off her rings and set them on the bedside table. The light scorched her eyes. She reached out and snapped it off, staring at the now-invisible rings until she had to blink.

At the door of their bedroom, he stopped. Without turning around, he said, "I'll help you pack in the morning. It'll work in our favor to separate now so it won't be such a surprise when I file for divorce."

Then he did turn, and his gaze sought hers. The hall light created a shadow of his broad shoulders against the carpet and obscured his face. "Is there anything I could have offered you that would have been worth reconsidering the divorce?"

Her throat cramped with grief. If she tried to talk, she'd break down, and every time she cried, he held her and made her feel things she shouldn't. Feelings he couldn't return.

When she didn't answer, he nodded and left.

In the darkness, she whispered, "You could have offered to love me."

Thirteen

The divorce papers sat on the edge of Lucas's desk, where they'd sat for a week now, without moving. Cia's loopy script was buried on the last page, where he couldn't see it. The papers lacked only his signature, but he couldn't sign. It didn't feel right. Nothing did. Certainly not his big, empty house, where he'd aimed to remove all traces of the previous couple who'd lived there and had succeeded beyond his wildest dreams.

Cia was everywhere. Sitting on the counter in the kitchen, eyes black with passion as he drove her to a brilliant climax. Walking down the stairs with careful steps, wearing a dress that had taken him an hour to find because none of the others would put appreciation on her face the way this exact one would.

Cia sleeping in his bed, hair tousled and flung across two pillows as she nestled right at the mattress's halfway mark, ripe for him to join her, to fold her against his body and sink in.

He groaned and slammed his head into his hands, ignoring the document filling the laptop screen before him.

That was the worst, trying to sleep alone after having Cia there, night after night. A blink in time, compared to how long he'd slept without her. But no matter how many times the maid washed the sheets, lime and coconut lingered in the creases, lying in wait to spring from hiding and invade his nose with the memory of what he'd lost.

No, not lost—what he'd never had in the first place.

He'd been wrong. Cia didn't need him. What could he say, what could he do, to counter that? If she didn't need him, he had no place in her life, as hard as that was to accept. She'd probably already whisked away whatever feelings she'd had for him, warm or otherwise.

At least he could bury himself in eighteen-hour days with no distractions and no one waiting at home.

All those closed-door sessions with Matthew had taken root. New clients vied for his attention. Contracts spilled from his workbag. Wheeler Family Partners for-sale signs dotted properties all across the city. The National Commercial Development Association had nominated WFP for an award—the highest percentage increase in listings for the year. Manzanares was icing on the cake.

Success and acknowledgment of his efforts. That's what he should be focusing on. Not on how every contract reminded him he should be closing the deal on his divorce and moving on. Every contract mocked him, silently asking why he couldn't just pick up a pen, for crying out loud.

He had to get out of here. Take a walk or a drive to clear his head. When he got back, he'd sign the papers and send them to his lawyer to be filed with the court. In no time, he'd be rid of this ache behind his ribs and free to pursue…something. Anything. The world was his for the taking.

But nothing interested him. At all.

He fingered the box in his pocket, which held Cia's rings.

It was time—past time—to stop carrying them around, but whenever he dug out the box and held it on his palm, his lungs cramped. The same cramp happened when he tried to remove his ring.

Maybe he should see a doctor. His throat hurt all the time. Some bug had probably wormed its way into his system.

When he rounded the corner to the reception area, Helena gave him her you-have-company-and-it's-not-a-client smile and said, "I was about to buzz you. You have a visitor."

Cia. His stomach flipped and a cold sweat broke out across his forehead. Maybe she'd thought it through and had recognized the excellent logic he'd so clearly laid out for why they belonged together.

Maybe she was pregnant. The image of her belly rounded with his child materialized in his head and pricked the backs of his eyes.

Or—he dragged his imagination back to the real world—she intended to flay him alive for not filing the papers yet. He pasted a smile on his face and pivoted to face the wrath of Hurricane Cia in full category-five mode.

He could never have prepared enough to greet the woman seated on the leather couch.

"Lana." *Not Cia.* Of course not. She'd never concede. He swallowed his disappointment. "This is a surprise."

"As it was meant to be. Hello, Lucas." Lana stood, balancing on delicate stilettos and clad in an expensive designer suit Cia would have sniffed at righteously.

Funny. He'd never noticed what Lana wore, other than to figure out the best way to get it off without ruining it, as she was ridiculously fussy about her clothes. Again, hindsight. Couldn't go home to her husband with buttons missing. "Is something wrong?"

With a glance at Helena, she said, "Can I buy you a cup of coffee?"

Yeah. Go out in public with Lana while still married to

Cia. Exactly what he needed. Actually, even a private conversation with Lana sounded less than fun, but as he took in the classy blonde who'd thanked him for his time and effort with lies, he realized he was over it.

And he was curious what she wanted. "Helena's coffee is better than any coffeehouse's. I have a few minutes. Let's sit in the conference room."

Lana followed him to the conference room across from the receptionist's desk, which he'd chosen due to the glass walls in case she thought there was a chance in hell he'd pick up where they'd left off.

He had a strong sense of propriety, not a shallow love for appearances as Cia liked to accuse him of.

Helena entered with two cups of coffee and left them on the table, along with an array of creamers and sugars. Lucas waited for Lana to take a seat and then chose a perpendicular chair.

"What can I do for you?" he asked politely.

Two artificial sweeteners and four creamers. Lana hadn't changed the way she drank coffee and likely nothing else, either. She took her time stirring, then looked up. "I came to apologize."

Lucas raised an eyebrow. "For which part?"

"All of it. I was lonely. Bored. Feeling adventurous. Take your pick. My shrink would agree with all of them. I'm not asking you to understand why I did it. Just to believe I'm sorry I hurt you."

"You didn't hurt me." He laughed and hated that it sounded forced. "You lied to me. You used me. Then you unleashed your husband on me to finish the evisceration job you started. That was the most unforgivable part."

He took a deep breath. Maybe he wasn't as over it as he'd imagined.

She sipped her coffee, as if for fortification, and blinked her baby blues. "I'm here to apologize for that, too," she said.

"And to tell you the truth. I didn't unleash my husband on you. All the rumors and hits to your business, I did that. Not Henry."

"What?" Shock froze his tongue, preventing him from voicing anything else. No. Not over it *at all*.

"Henry will be fifty-eight in December. I had no illusions about being in love when I married him and neither did he. When I told him about you, he patted my hand and said it was cheaper than a divorce, then went back to work. I played him up as the jealous husband because, well, I wanted you to believe I had worth to him."

"Why?" he prompted when she paused.

"Because you're so hard to faze, Lucas. Emotionally. Do you feel anything at all? I wanted you to love me and you didn't. I thought…maybe if you believed he loved me, you'd see something desirable in me, too. Only it didn't work. I was heartbroken. Devastated that it was just all fun and games to you."

"It was fun," he reminded her harshly. She had a lot of nerve, talking about love when they'd been nowhere near serious. "It could have been more, maybe. Eventually. At least, I thought it could."

Genuine sadness laced her small smile. "Could have been. Maybe. Eventually. That's how it is with you. No commitment. So I lashed out. Tried to ruin you. Instead, you fell in love with someone else, blew past all my efforts to destroy you and went on to be happy without me."

A catch in her throat cut off the sentence and a catch in his gut kept his resounding "No" from being voiced.

He wasn't happy.

The rest of it was true. He was in love with Cia, and he needed her, like a tree needed water. She brought out all the best parts of him and kept him on his toes. She challenged him and made him feel alive.

He'd given her up, so sure that if she didn't need him, they had no reason to be together.

Ironic how Lana hadn't accused him of marrying Cia on the rebound after all. Instead, she'd put a microscope on his marriage, and the view shook his spine something fierce.

She coughed and touched a finger to the corner of her eye. "I'm sorry, and I'm not going to bother you anymore. I'm in a place now where I can be happy for you."

And he was in a place where he could accept Lana had cut him deeper than he'd been willing to admit, spilling over into his relationship with Cia and causing missteps visible only in hindsight. *Hindsight.* The word of the day.

"Okay." He stood so fast the rolling chair shot away from the backs of his legs. "Thanks for coming by. You didn't have to, and I appreciate it."

Surprised, she glanced up. "Rushing me out? I guess I don't blame you. Good luck, Lucas. You deserve a much better life than what I could have given you."

In his head, the word *life* became *wife*. He agreed. He deserved a better wife than one who betrayed him the way Lana had. But his wife deserved a better husband than one who had betrayed her. Like he'd done to Cia. He'd done all she'd accused him of, and more, and probably not as subconsciously as he'd insisted.

He'd refused to see the truth. He'd been so busy trying to have what Matthew had had that he'd missed the most critical element. It was clear now why his brother hadn't been able to live in the house he'd built with Amber, why he'd taken off despite being a Wheeler.

Love made a person do crazy, irrational things. Things he'd never do under normal circumstances, like offer a short-term wife millions of dollars to make it long-term. Instead of blowing off Cia's broken heart like a complete moron, he should have just opened his mouth and admitted he wanted to alter the deal because he loved her and couldn't live without her.

It might not have changed the outcome. But it might have.
Love. That was the reason he couldn't move on this time.
He'd been too afraid of it, too much a coward to examine what
he was feeling, and it would serve him right to have lost Cia
forever. But he wasn't going down without a fight.

He hurried to his office to start on the Lucas Wheeler
Philosophy of Cia Wheeler. He had to get it right this time.

Something was wrong with Fergie. Cia had tried everything, but the bird wouldn't eat. The blob of gray feathers
sat in the bottom of the cage and refused to acknowledge
the presence of her owner. It had been like this since the day
she'd moved back into her condo.

Every morning, she rushed to Fergie's cage, convinced
she'd find the bird claws up and stiff with rigor mortis, which
would be about right for a companion she'd anticipated having for fifty years.

One more thing ripped from her fingers.

"You have to eat sometime," she told Fergie. Not that she
blamed her. Cia had no appetite, either, and after cooking in
Amber's gourmet kitchen, the one in her condo, which she'd
been using for years, wasn't the same. "We'll try again tomorrow."

At quarter till nine, she went to bed, where she would
likely not sleep because she refused to turn on the TV and
refused to acknowledge she'd grown used to it.

She didn't need the TV, and she didn't need Lucas Wheeler.
For anything, least of all to "help" her find another shelter site.
She had an internet connection and lots of patience. Okay,
maybe not so much patience. Tomorrow she'd investigate
using another real estate professional. A female.

Cia stared at the dark ceiling and shifted for the hundredth
time into yet another uncomfortable spot on the hard mattress. It was just so quiet without the TV. Without the rustle

of sheets and the deep breathing of a warm, male body scant inches away.

Not a night went by without a stern internal reminder of how much better it was to be alone, instead of constantly looking over her shoulder for the guillotine that would sever her happiness.

A knock at the front door interrupted her misery. Grumbling, she threw on a robe and flipped on a light as she crossed the small condo. A peek through the peephole shot her pulse into the stratosphere.

Lucas.

With a sheaf of papers in his hand. The divorce papers. He was dropping them off—personally—this late?

Hands shaking, she unlatched the door and swung it open. "What are you doing here?"

"Hello to you, too." He captured her gaze, flooding her with a blue tidal wave of things unsaid. Unresolved.

The porch light shone down, highlighting his casual dress. Cargoes and a T-shirt, which meant he hadn't come straight from work. Was he not working all hours of the night anymore? Dark splotches under his eyes and lines of fatigue in his forehead told a different tale.

She set her back teeth together. She had to get out of the habit of caring.

"Come in, before I let in all the mosquitoes in Uptown." She stepped back and allowed him to brush past her, to prove his raw Lucas-ness didn't have any power here. His heat warmed her suddenly chilled skin, and the quick tug in her abdomen made a liar out of her.

A squawk stopped his progress midstride. Fergie flapped her wings and ran back and forth along one of the wooden dowels anchored across the top of her cage. "Lucas, Lucas, Lucas," she singsonged.

Cia glared at her miraculously revived bird. "I didn't know she could say that."

"Took her long enough." He grinned, and his eyes lit up. All the butterflies in her stomach took flight. "We've been working on it."

So. Fergie and Lucas had been buddy-buddy behind her back. She sighed. Maybe Fergie would eat, now that her precious Lucas was here. Traitor.

She waved at the couch. "Sit down."

He sank into the giant white sectional, and it shrank as his frame dominated the space. Then he spilled his masculinity into the rest of the room, overwhelming her.

Why had he come here, invading her refuge?

Luckily, he'd had the wisdom to move them into Matthew's house—his house now—instead of moving in here for the duration. The separation would have been a hundred times more difficult if she'd had to wash his presence from the condo. No way she could have. She would've had to move.

Might still have to, just from this visit.

"Will you sit with me?" He nodded to the couch.

"I prefer to stand, thanks. Besides, you're not staying long. Are you dropping off the papers?"

"In a way," he said. "But first, I'd like to tell you something. You know my great-great-grandfather founded Wheeler Family Partners back in the eighteen hundreds, right?"

When she nodded, he went on, "Back then, there weren't many buildings. Mostly land. That's true real estate, and it's in my blood. I used to think real estate was about deals. A piece of paper, signed and filed. Then I was done, ready to move on to the next deal. But that's not who I am anymore. I'm in the business of partnering with people to build something real. Something permanent. That's why I grew WFP without Matthew. Not because I got lucky or worked hard. I fell in love with someone who challenges me to be more. Who taught me the value of wholehearted commitment."

¡Dios mío!

"Is *that* where you were going?" She laughed, and it came

out more like a sob. So now he was in love with her. Conveniently. "You came to deliver divorce papers and tell me you decided you're in love with me. Anything else?"

He came off the couch in a rush, feet planted and eyes blazing. Involuntarily, she backed up from the heat of his anger. *This* was Lucas mad. Before, by the pool, was nothing in comparison.

"I'm not here to deliver divorce papers." He held them up and flicked his other hand. A lighter appeared between his fingers, flame extended.

Before she could blink, he set the papers on fire.

Smoke curled away from the burning pages, and her divorce deal turned to ash. He blew out the fire before it reached his fingers and threw the charred corners on her pristine coffee table, metal glinting from his third finger with the motion. He was still wearing his wedding ring.

"What did you do that for?" she demanded, pulse pounding. "I have a copy in the other room, and you're not leaving here until you sign it."

His taut frame still bristled as he dismissed the demand with a curt slice of his hand. "I am not divorcing you. Period." He took a deep, steadying breath. "Cia, listen for a minute. I handled it all wrong. I'm sorry. I cut down what mattered most to you and undermined your goals with the shelter, trying to force you to need me. I was too much of a dingbat to realize I'd done everything except the one thing you really wanted."

"Oh, what's that?" she asked. Tears stabbed at her eyes, burned down her throat.

"You stuck your heart out and then yanked it right back so quickly, I almost didn't see it. You don't give a guy a chance to think about what to do with such a gift, and I'm sorry it took me so long to figure out what would be enough." He inched toward her slowly, giving her time to move. Or to stay. "You want someone to love you. You want *me* to love you."

Her lungs contracted as his heart splashed onto his face.

This was definitely not some conveniently discovered feeling calculated to get his way. He'd never looked at her with such fierce longing coupled with aching tenderness.

And yet, he'd always looked at her like that. She'd never dared examine it. Never dared hope it meant more than warm feelings for the woman he was sleeping with.

When he'd taken all the steps he could, she hadn't moved. He swept her up in his arms.

"Darlin'," he whispered into her hair. "Let me love you."

She shut her eyes and breathed in Lucas. Breathed in the acrid, charred scent of burned paper as his body cleaved to hers and he held her. It would be so easy to plunge into this new Lucas, the one who opened up and poured out poetry and promises like sap from a felled tree.

With her stomach and heart twisting, she broke his embrace. "That's not what I want."

"Stop pretending." Ferocity leaped back into his expression. "You're so afraid, you either fake everything or you fight it, as if that will insulate you from hurt. Nothing will. But being alone hurts in a different way."

His blue laser beams punched right through her, past the flesh and bone. She'd struggled so hard to be whole, to heal from losing pieces of her soul. First, when her parents died and after, when she tried to replace the loss with disastrous relationships.

And here she was, with no empty space. No room for anyone, not even this surprising, layered man who stood before her, asking for something she couldn't give.

"I am afraid." Had she said that out loud?

"I know, honey. I know all about fear. Do you think it was easy for me to come here with nothing to give except myself? Jewelry and spectacular sex are much easier to offer than risking you'll accept plain old me. But I'm hoping it's enough, because I can't live my life without you."

He was saying all the right things. Except he was first and

foremost a salesman, and she'd experienced his stellar ability to sell himself firsthand. "You wanted me to be needy. But not anymore?"

"Yeah. I wanted you to need me and told myself fulfilling your needs was my half of the partnership. A total lie. It was so I didn't have to do the work. So I could keep from investing emotionally. The worst part is, I was already in deep and couldn't tell you how much I need *you*. You're right. Need is dangerous." He inclined his head in deference. "I can't survive without you. I'm completely addicted to you. And I love you too much to let you go."

The sentiment darted right through her flimsy barriers and spread with warmth into the emptiness she would have sworn wasn't there.

Lucas had known, though, and burrowed right past the pretense, past all the lies she told herself. It was frightening to consider just being real for once and more frightening still to consider giving up her defenses. "How can I know for sure this isn't all going to evaporate one day?"

"I don't have a crystal ball. All I have is right here." He held his hands wide, palms up. "Can you forgive me?"

She shut her eyes against the raw emotion spilling from the sea of blue trained on her face. No sales pitch there. Just a whole lot of Lucas, showing her the inner reaches of his heart. "This is a lot to take in. Without the divorce, I don't get my money. How can I live with that?"

His expression grew cunning. "How can you live with yourself if you do get your money? You don't want to be a slave to need, yet you're willing to be one to your grandfather."

She flinched. "What are you talking about?"

"You're dependent on your grandfather and his money to grant you a measure of control over a life that can't be controlled." He advanced on her, backing her up until she hit the wall. "I'm not above stacking the deck to get what

I want, and I want you, Cia Wheeler. I dare you to take a risk on us. I dare you to stare your grandfather in the eye and tell him to keep his money, because you're keeping your marriage."

Vocalized in Lucas's whiskey-smooth voice, her name sounded beautiful. Exactly right. It was too much. He saw too much, wanted too much. He made her want too much.

"How can I?" she whispered.

"Simple. You have needs, whether you like it or not. They're part of being human, so you have to make a choice. Do you need your grandfather to take care of you financially? Or do you need to take a chance on a new deal with me? A mutually beneficial deal, because, honey, you need me as much as I need you. The question is, can you admit it?"

There it was. He'd drawn the line, given her a choice. Maybe it was that easy to just say *yes*. But it couldn't be. "What if I don't want kids?"

He flashed a grin. "What if I do? What if I don't want you to keep a single stitch of your wardrobe? What if I want to put on clown makeup and join the circus? What if—"

"Okay. I get it." And he got her. Not so difficult to believe after all, not when it was Lucas. That's why the betrayal had hurt so much, because he'd twisted the knife with expert knowledge. "You're saying we'll figure it out."

"Together. I love you and that will never change. It's the only guarantee I've got. Well, I can also guarantee we'll fight over the radio station. But I'm willing to overlook your terrible taste in music if it means I get a real wife out of the deal. Do I?"

Real. Everything she'd been afraid to want until Lucas. The divorce deal was a flawed shield against a real relationship, but fear of losing something meaningful had squelched all her courage to reach for that dream.

She'd done her best to get rid of Lucas before he could hurt her, but he kept coming back. Maybe it was finally time to stop fighting it. Time to admit she loved him fiercely.

Could she take a chance on a marriage deal? Could she risk the possibilities, bad or good?

"No." Mind made up, she inspected him through narrowed eyes and crossed her arms. "How is that fair? You get a real wife in exchange for exposure to my excellent taste in music. Yet I'll be forced to listen to songs about cheating, honky-tonks and cheap beer? No deal. Find a pen and sign the copy of the papers right now unless you can agree to find a type of music we both like."

His gaze played over her face, and when he smiled, the sun rose. No point in denying it. She'd given a huge piece of her heart to Lucas a long time ago, and he was offering to fill that hole with himself. Love had healed her, and now, she could let him do that.

"Opera?" he suggested and yanked her into his arms, engulfing her in the scent of clean pine. The scent of her real husband.

His mouth captured hers before she could argue opera was more a type of theater than a type of music. Lucas kissed her, and her heart became whole, then swelled, too big for her chest.

She pulled back a tiny bit, unwilling to be too far from him. "I really, really hope you meant it when you said you love me, because if you want a real wife, you're going to have to suffer through a big, formal wedding. And I'm asking your mother to help plan it."

He groaned. "I meant it. You know you'll have to suffer through a real honeymoon in exchange, right?"

"With lots of real sex? *Dios,* the things I do for you." With a tsk, she smiled. "I must love you a lot."

"Well, then. Since we're already married, the big, formal wedding is merely symbolic. So the honeymoon comes first." He peeled back her robe and rolled his eyes at the tank top underneath. "Please. I'm begging you. Let me buy you some nice, tasteful sleepwear not made from cotton."

"Not unless you let me teach you to dance." His hands slid under the tank top and claimed her body, just like he'd claimed her heart. "Lucas," she breathed.

Fergie squawked, "Lucas, Lucas, Lucas."

Lucas laughed against Cia's mouth. "That's a deal."

Even with Fran's help, the wedding plans stretched over the course of two months. The real story was far too incredible, so Lucas smoothed over everyone's questions with the partial truth—Cia'd had a change of heart about including everyone in their marriage celebration, and she wanted a lavish second ceremony.

Finally, after endless rounds of making decisions and sampling cake and addressing invitations, Cia clutched Abuelo's arm and walked down the aisle to her husband. Then, nearly five hundred guests accompanied them to an extravagant reception, where the bride and groom danced to every song, be it fast or slow.

Lucas twirled Cia to one of his favorite country numbers and she sang along, not ashamed to admit she kind of liked it, twangy guitars and all. He gathered her close and smiled. "Was it worth it? The big wedding?"

"It's everything I dreamed it would be. Exhausting but so wonderful."

That morning, she'd begun to suspect the exhaustion wasn't due to frantic wedding plans but another reason entirely. But she'd had no time to slip away and buy a pregnancy test. Tomorrow was soon enough to confirm it.

She couldn't wait to find out for sure. A whole, intact heart allowed for plenty of possibilities, and, finally, she was in a place where the thought of a baby didn't scare her blind. And if the test came back negative, they'd try some more. It was all in the journey and the pleasures to be had along the way.

When the music ended, Lucas escorted her to the table, and Fran flashed yet another proud smile. Cia touched the pearls around her neck and grinned at Fran and Andy in turn. She'd gained a family along with a husband.

Well, most of a family—Matthew hadn't come back for the wedding and it weighed on Lucas. Hopefully she could cheer him up tomorrow with the news he'd started on the next generation of Wheelers a little earlier than expected.

Abuelo approached the table and took Cia's hand. "I'm afraid this old man must retire for the evening, my dear. Lucas, I'll be in your office a week from Monday to sign the papers. I'm a little sad to see the Manzanares complex change hands, but I couldn't be happier with the deal you negotiated."

"Anything for family. I'm glad to be of service." Lucas clasped Abuelo's outstretched hand and wished him a good evening.

Only after a knockdown, drag-out fight, which Cia refused to lose, had Lucas agreed to still represent Abuelo in the sale of Manzanares, even though he hadn't followed through with the divorce. Seriously, her husband took integrity to a whole new level. When Cia pointed out she couldn't trust any other real estate broker with Abuelo's business except Lucas, he conceded.

Abuelo hadn't budged on changing the terms of the trust, despite Cia's zealous pleas, but she was okay with that. In lieu of wedding gifts, Cia and Lucas had asked for donations to the newly formed Wheeler Family Foundation, helmed quite expertly by Fran Wheeler, and the balance grew by leaps and bounds daily.

Every time Cia launched into an impassioned explanation about the work she and Fran were doing, and every time someone handed her another check, she could feel her mother smiling down in approval. Nothing could bring back her parents, but trusting Lucas with her heart had finally allowed Cia to close that chapter and embrace the next one.

She dreamed of forever, and Lucas Wheeler was exactly the man to give it to her.

* * * * *